D0905075

For my father, Victor Fischmann,
Parisian Jew, disciple of Groucho Marx
and Jean Jaurès.

For my mother, Ida Carmen Haïk who
breathed with the Kabbalah.

For Yvette and Lucien Fayman.

I dedicate this feast of stories
In full celebration of everything they were:
    sincere and bountiful,
Drawing upon glints that have been
    lost from
The harried light.

Jewish Stories
of Wisdom

Translation copyright © 2016 Black Dog & Leventhal Publishers

First published in France under the title *Contes des sages Juifs* by
Patrick Fishmann © 2013, Éditions du Seuil

Black Dog & Leventhal Publishers
Hachette Book Group
1290 Avenue of the Americas
New York, NY 10104
www.blackdogandleventhal.com

Printed in China

IM

First Edition: February 2016
10 9 8 7 6 5 4 3 2 1

Black Dog & Leventhal Publishers is an imprint of Hachette Books,
a division of Hachette Book Group. The Black Dog & Leventhal
Publishers name and logo are trademarks of Hachette Book Group, Inc.

The Hachette Speakers Bureau provides a wide range of authors for
speaking events. To find out more, go to www.HachetteSpeakersBureau.
com or call (866) 376-6591.

The publisher is not responsible for websites (or their content) that are
not owned by the publisher.

Library of Congress Cataloging-in-Publication Data available
upon request.

ISBN: 978-0-31634-994-9

Jewish Stories of Wisdom

PATRICK FISCHMANN

Translated by Vivien Groves

BLACK DOG
& LEVENTHAL
PUBLISHERS
NEW YORK

Contents

Overture

I t all begins with this strange and very
Jewish story.

There were some words trotting along
a road in search of a thought capable of
making a man's mouth sing or a book dance.

This was so that they might cultivate
the world together and renew it.

And that they might disclose each face,
for it to question and understand itself.

And remember its future. *Olam Habba.*

A story revealed during a *paper vigil,*
composed of words accompanied by music,
dancing with the joys and sorrows of this
world, within the peace of a thought that
learns for itself. Woven by the letters that
create existence, and replying, *Hineni, I am
ready, I am here*: a story to ensure that the
Promised Land feels at home in it.

11

Derived from the *aggadot* and the Jewish soul: a universal friend.

So that it might be *the song that inhabits the song*, as articulated by Elie Wiesel.

Or Franz Kafka's art of prayer: *a hand stretched out into the darkness wanting to grasp a share of mercy in order to change into a giving hand.*

The Veils
of the Torah

The Lord had imparted much knowledge to gems, plants, and animals. The lapis lazuli, the blue cedar, and the green woodpecker, like all the creatures, knew what they were talking about. Barely hatched, the frigate bird remembered the courtship ritual that the Lord had entrusted to it. The butterfly emerged from its place of darkness in a wedding gown. Man arrived, woven in oblivion. He had to seek, venture, and accomplish. He had to liberate and gather together the sparks of light scattered in the Creation. Thus he received "the handkerchief on which the Shekhinah had written thousands of tightly spaced letters with her tears—the handkerchief belonging to the Torah of the Jewish people."* In the depths of the sacred cloth that "conceals the glow of its face," a drop as vast as an ocean was shining.

It had the color of exile and an unfathomable holiness.

Storytellers are blessed four times. They are steeped in this tear, obliterated and lulled, infused, and cleansed by the waves. They are traversed by the fire of the word and subdued by the breath. They gather the smiles and the tears across the faces of their fellows that are invited to the feast. See the gift that they have received: They study day and night to liberate and assemble stories.

* Pietro Citati, *The Exile of the Shekhinah.*

Which of the Three: The Three

*Every Wisdom and Intellect has its own
specific tune and melody.*
Rabbi Nahman of Bratslav

Three Jews were walking along the road,
holding forth as was their custom,
speaking loudly and arguing as they jostled
each other with little asides, not to be right, but
to invigorate their health. They did their best
to sprinkle the manifold and paradoxical word
of the living God with their disagreements.
It should be said that they were hoping to be
baffled by the hidden meaning of things, to be
overwhelmed by doubt, and to fish for some
new idea springing forth from the void. They
had gotten to know each other in the same
house of study and continued to keep the flame
of contention and friendship burning. They

had not yet entered into marriage—one was a cabinetmaker, the second a tailor, and the third studied the Talmud and the Kabbalah.

They had been debating a noteworthy subject ever since they had left Touggourt: *When should one keep quiet and when is it prudent to speak?*

"My master said that if you really converse with the wood that you plane, you can only hear the voice of the planer in the studio."

"Perhaps this is because he had nothing to say to the wood. For my part, I speak to my fabrics because I want them to know."

"Doesn't the mind more readily whisper to us to be quiet when one has something to say?"

"Better to become mute than be silent for show!"

"The master thought it was the wood that was teaching the cabinetmaker and that if the pupil thinks he's the master, the plank of wood would never be able to keep quiet or shout."

"I have never heard a single fabric interrupt me!"

"Isn't it better to cut the cloth, and keep quiet so that it can express what you create?"

Bara bara bara, they started singing, *create, create, create*—a song they had composed themselves during their years at the house of study that would bring the blessed squabbling to an end at supper time. As they reached the edge of the desert and the sun hugged the horizon, each friend found himself more or less in agreement with the silence of the other two to camp there. They ate everything as they discussed who would take the first, second, and third watch. The cabinetmaker was chosen to cover the first part of the night. He was appointed because he had an odd habit of wanting to carve a figure out of wood from the forest before he fell asleep. The scholar, who got up before sunrise each morning, was entrusted with the third watch of the night. The tailor, whose craft comprised cutting and assembling pieces of cloth, was offered the position of the scissors and the needle, between the first watch and the third watch. As the world order was safe,

they thought it would be better to wake the other two if the Messiah arrived, rather than have to herald the presence of a wild animal or a gang of bandits.

As his two friends were starting to doze, the cabinetmaker was contemplating the sparks produced by the night's fire. The crackling of the wood seemed like the joyous song of a tree journeying back from exile. As he picked up a log, he noticed a piece of olive tree. It was slightly big, but it had a beautiful natural curve and an unctuous smoothness, and it would have been a waste to burn it. He took his tools out of his bag and let himself be guided by the sapwood. He soon became aware that his chisel was revealing the contours of a woman. Four hours later, the beauty was vibrant, and the fire danced only for her. The cabinetmaker shook the tailor's shoulder and lay down, contented.

When the tailor broke free of his lethargy and the ghostly images of his dreams, he saw the woman carved from wood and thought that his friend was undoubtedly a true artist. He had imparted the shape and the taste of paradise to something that did not exist. As he had pieces of cloth, thread, pins, and needles in his haversack, he thought that to clothe the princess of the night would honor beauty, and his friend. The Milky Way gave him the basic idea and the Great Bear blew a gentle breeze to feed his imagination. He busied himself cutting, trying the pieces of cloth on her for size, and sewing. Four hours later, the woman made of wood was clothed. The tailor stretched, and whispered in the third friend's ear that it was his turn to keep watch.

Before he opened his eyes, the kabbalist murmured *Modé ani léfanékha,* the morning prayer; then he got up, took out his book, and put on his *talith*. Quickly absorbed by contemplation, he nevertheless was conscious of music filtering through him that was unknown to his meditation, making it if not exotic, at least unfamiliar. He raised his eyes and saw the woman roused from her night of wood and prepared for the dance of life. As a mystic, he knew that the stories about Golem preferred to make reference to ecstatic joys than to awakened statues. But . . . it flashed across his mind that one might be able to bring the woman of wood to life through intense prayer and the magic of the prose. He felt that he had to put the finishing touches to what his companions had undertaken. With his eyes closed, he whispered the formulae his masters had taught him and then decided against it, with letters of fire and unknown words streaming into him.

When he opened his eyes again, the statue had become a woman, and his friends had woken, alerted by the marvel. The three bachelors were amazed, won over by a mixture of love and shock with their hearts endorsing the maxim: *a joyful heart is a woman.* She stepped forward and said:

"Half for one of you and the other for God. Who will give me their hand?"

"If the cabinetmaker hadn't made you, we wouldn't have known you," said the scholar.

" ... but if the tailor hadn't hidden your beauty, wouldn't the kabbalist have gone mad?"

"Yes, I have made you a skin, but the kabbalist snatched you from oblivion. The cabinetmaker made you naked so that I might clothe you; the scholar has roused you so that my pieces of cloth serve some purpose. Decide."

The woman started to laugh.

"I desire it to be according to your wishes."

Her silhouette glided to the left and disclosed the forms of two more women. They were like three sisters, and each one was like the other. However, they were different since each of the three friends knew which woman suited his heart.

The Possibility Shall Be Offered

He that dwelleth in the secret place
of the most High shall abide under
the shadow of the Almighty.
Book of David, Psalm 91,1

Rabbi Akiva, a former shepherd who had become a master, had set out on a journey to sustain the courage of the Jews of North Africa and the East, in the face of the Roman oppressor. He traveled with an absolute confidence in life, which he thought was prescribed and blessed by the most High, whatever occurred and despite appearances. When ordinary mortals revolted against adversity and clenched a vengeful fist, he opened his hand to them and uttered his prayer: *Everything is for the best.*

Crossing a town, he asked the people if they could give him shelter for the night.

But the passers-by turned away, leaving the *tzadik* to roam, with no response other than avoidance and scorn. However, one of them tarried and said to him in a provocative way:

"I believe that your God is going to leave you on your own this night to sleep under the stars with a pillow of stone."

"May he welcome me into his fields," replied the wise man. "This arid garden suits me, as it is planted with the grass of justice and goodness."

He went past the last of the hovels and entered the fields with their sweet and bitter grasses. When the sun went down, he lit his lamp and felt good about himself. Tomorrow, the cockerel he had brought with him would wake him with his crowing at daybreak, and his donkey would carry him to his next destination. He fell asleep peacefully.

But that night, a strong gust of wind extinguished his lamp, a wild cat ate his cockerel, and a starving lion devoured his donkey. Woken by the gust of wind and the screaming of the animals, alone in total darkness, he put his hand in the grass of justice and goodness, and murmured, "Everything is for the best." Then he improvised a kind of poem.

I know what I have to do, and I do it
But I know what I do not know!
Beyond my understanding
Everything contributes to goodness
In the fields of the most High,
Of Ra'hamana the Merciful,
My lamp has gone out,
My cockerel and my donkey have been
  eaten,
No rancor can be poured out
Into a heart overflowing with love.

At that moment, he could hear shouting coming from the inhospitable town. A gang of bandits had attacked it and was conquering it. He stroked the ground and took up the refrain silently to himself.

Without the wind, blown through your
  lips

My lamp would have shone in the night.
Without the savagery of your teeth
My cockerel would have crowed and my
    donkey would have brayed.
Without the two grasses and the two
    faces of the One True God
The cavalrymen would have captured me!
I know what I have to do, and I do it
But I know what I do not know!
Beyond my understanding
Everything contributes to goodness.

In the morning, he went on his way again, murmuring, *A col tsafoui be a rechout netouna*: everything is anticipated or possible, and the possibility shall be offered.

To Whom Does
the Future Belong?

*... to those who will have the
longest memory.*
The Baal Shem Tov

While the Jewish people were sleeping,
a sweet child came into the world
and was imbued with the wise teachings of
his first masters: the trees and the birds. Who
was the best able to encourage the boy to
study—who, if not the assembly of the wise
men of the forest, his first *yeshiva*? Inspired
by the song of the earth, invigorated by the
breeze and under the benevolent eye of the
pine trees, he placed the manuscripts of the
Kabbalah on the moss—these treasures kept
by the hidden Tzadikim. Listening to the
cheerful birds, he could see that penance was
unnecessary. Their joyous trills encircled

each dance of life. They brought back sorrows
into their world in tender waves. Even if
a disaster occurred in the forests, a finch
chirped the elation of the Lord, interlacing
life. Through the song of a bird, he invited
humanity to delight at the very depths of the
tribulation, sublimating all the sorrows of the
world. The man who would later perform
miracles and marvels, the Master of the
Good Name Baal Shem Tov, was filling up
with the teachings drawn from our mother

nature. *He was putting oil in his lamp,* for all the years to come.

Most of the things known about him were related by his disciples. One day, one of his disciples, who was much loved by the Baal Shem Tov, came to him with the intention of obtaining a favor. He was put off by the uncustomarily distant reception of the master, who did, however, invite him to accompany him. The rabbi's silence increasingly concerned him.

"Do you think I am unaware of what you have on your mind, eh?"

The disciple shuddered like an open book through whose pages the wise man was leafing.

"You have come so that I can teach you the language of the birds, eh, is that all?"

The disciple silently nodded in agreement.

While letting himself be carried by the rhythm of the carriage, the rabbi revealed the secret wisdom to the disciple; he unsealed *the corks driven into his ears.* The disciple, dumbfounded, discovered the meaning of the conversations in which the thrushes perched on the tree branches engaged. He was propelled into another dimension where everything seemed topsy-turvy, where each moment was an act of praise carried by the creature, like this sparrow song that whispered a motif, able to revolutionize the exegeses of doctors of the Law. When they reached their destination, the master passed his hand over the disciple's face, erasing from his memory the gift he did not possess.

"If you were predestined to it, I would have revealed the magical language. This is not the case. Therefore, serve the Lord with the means at your disposal, and search the oldest memory that you can find, for yourself."

It is said that when the Baal Shem Tov had to confront a delicate situation, he went to a spot in the forest, which was a unique place to make a fire and pray. What had befitted him to accomplish occurred, even if it were a miracle. Time passed. A generation later, the Maggid of

Mezeritch did likewise. He went to the same place to pray. He didn't know how to light the fire, but remembered some words and was able to say the prayer. And what had befitted him to accomplish occurred, even if it were a miracle. Time passed, and a generation later the Rabbi Moshe Lev of Sasov also went to sit there. He could not remember how to light the fire or the exact words of the prayer or how to say it. But he remembered the place. Yes, what had befitted him to accomplish occurred, even if it were a miracle. Much later on, it was the turn of Rabbi Israel de Rijn. At that time, so many threats menaced the Jews. He sat in his abode, on his beautiful chair, and with his head between his hands fervently beseeched the angel of memory. He did not know anything—how to light the fire, or remember the words, or the intonations to recite the prayer, or the place in which it was wise to say it. He only remembered one thing: this story. And what had befitted him to accomplish occurred, even if it were a miracle.

I am here, in your presence, unaware of the magical places known by the *tzadikim*, with my damp matches and my moist wood, my incoherent words and my wandering thoughts. I am here, quick to lose my concentration, suffering from not knowing the magic words that open the windows of the sky. But I am the guardian of this story; I intend to accomplish my lofty mission so the miracle does not disappear.

The Poet
and the Pirate

Abraham ibn Ezra, who was a scholar, an eminent poet, and a *tzadik,* was also a gifted storyteller. He transported his audience into the heart of things with simplicity and humor, seeking the path of gentleness. As his words were a living source, he flipped malcontents over like pancakes, and in truth this good magic made this Jew from Cordoba into a renowned, but very poor, wise man. He had tried his hand at many trades but accepted the evidence: whatever he undertook, he found that only poetry, science, and the practice of wisdom were fundamental and prospered. All his other undertakings foundered. He smiled about it: *If I made candles, the sun would no longer set, and if I sold shrouds, the people would stop dying.* Thus, what could he do if not travel, to be true to himself, in order to offer what he had to provide? He left Cordoba with the blessing of the people—in order to travel across the world.

He arrived on foot in a Mediterranean port and boarded a merchant ship bound for Morocco. On the first night he watched the sky, the chart of which he was familiar with, having studied it in treatises on Greek, Persian, Hindu, and Arabic astronomy and astrology and taken notes for his own observations. The second night was devoted to prayer and reflection. At the end of another day, the serene moon made its appearance surrounded by a disquieting halo. In the middle of the night, amid a confusion of screams and sounds of struggle, the boat was boarded and captured by pirates.

At dawn, their leader spoke harshly to the merchants and prisoners lined up on the deck. He was ugly, showing the scars of a dissolute life, but his eyes shone with extraordinary brightness.

"Let's see whether you can afford to purchase your lives! Empty your bags, your trunks, and your pockets for me! I will show no mercy."

Per hanc portam ingressi
sunt primium Lusita: qui
hoc oppidum

A cloth merchant was relieved of his
cargo, and thrown into the sea for his
obvious poverty. Trembling intensely,
a banker took out his chest of gold and
followed the fate of the merchant, as he had
only brought gratuities with him, unworthy
of the bandits. The condemnations came
thick and fast, interspersed with dry
laughter and distributing the booty. Seven
others followed the same fate—they were

tradesmen, prominent people, and grocers. A rich man with trunks full of jewels and gold was accused of having left the main part of his fortune at home and was sent to the back.

"Ah, there remains a Jew," said the leader. "Not really a prince, but do we ever know? What do you have to offer us apart from your bedside book and your old shawl?"

"I'm afraid there's nothing I can offer you that will please you. My treasures are made from a material that only sings to pirates with intellect."

"Throw the pillager into the water!"

"Shut your mouths," said the leader. "He pleases me, he's plucky. We really should have a bit of fun. Are you one . . . of these pirates with intellect?"

"Yes."

"And what does that amount to?"

Abraham ibn Ezra had not been able to escape the gaze of the leader's burning eyes, and observed that they were becoming brighter. Despite his difficult situation, his curiosity about the human soul was intact and he wondered what quest was hiding behind this rapacious gaze.

"This amounts to knowing how to die as one has lived, as a poet. Allow me to say farewell to this life that I have loved so much, so that I might send the gold from my heart and my head flying among the waves."

And the poet moved forward across the deck and recited.

My friends, take my hand
Now that my faith burns like a fire,
And the departure of the graceful fawn of
*   my love*
Fills my eyes with bitter tears,
And this resonant dew escapes from them,
Overcoming the silence.

"Tell me, pirate of intellect, would you harbor good riddles? I myself am aware that viziers and sultans envy me that. I know the price of things. I can steal all the gold from every ship, but words from the intellect have an inestimable value that my hand alone could not reach. You can question my crew; I would give anything, at each port, to find the person who would lodge in my bandit's brain a riddle worthy of this name. Catch me out, impress the expert that I am, and your life will be spared."

Ibn Ezra had to find the implacable riddle immediately. He retreated quietly into himself as if to buy some time, while a tiny Abraham visited his memories at the speed of light. At last he smiled; he had found it.

41

"It's a battlefield where there's no soil, no cries, and not a single drop of blood is shed. It's a king without a prince or scepter; it's a queen with no jewels or a silky dress; horses without riders and riders without weapons; valets with no feet, and the jesters there are mute; the towers have no windows. What is it?"

The pirate ordered that the poet should be treated like a guest, and should be fed and allowed to get some rest. The pirate sat to one side and all traces of harshness were erased from his face. He could have been taken for a child who was searching for the solution to a problem. The noise of his men pouring out drinks as they broke open the barrels, singing loudly, didn't seem to reach his ears. Night descended, and he was still there with his eyes raised toward the sky and his heart in his mouth. The night turned into morning. At the end of the afternoon, he called Abraham over and conceded defeat.

"Well?"

"The battlefield where there's no soil,

no cries, and not a single drop of blood is shed, is the chessboard. All the others—the king without a prince or scepter, the queen with no jewels, the valets with no feet, the mute jesters, and the towers with no windows—are the chess pieces.

The pirate shook his head with admiration.

The following day, he dropped the wise man off along the shore and gave him a full purse as a present.

Thus began the first voyage of Abraham ibn Ezra. As he walked along, he savored the life he loved so much.

If I had wings of a dove,
I would fly without stopping
Until I had laid my eyes on the fawn
That eclipses the sun.

The Language of Shlomo

S hlomo, the wisest man among wise men,
understood the language of animals and
birds. He had derived true humility from
this intimate knowledge. It was by listening
to them conversing, and by talking amicably
to the swallow, the lioness, and the eagle that
he had grasped the profound nature of each
creature and experienced in the depths of his
soul the extent of the folly of pride.

One day when he was talking to the
queen ant, he suddenly became angry. She
claimed to be larger than him and he had
hurled her to the ground.

"Believe me, Shlomo, the Lord has
placed me in your hand to warn you and I
do it solemnly from the soil of Israel: It is
forbidden for a creature of flesh and blood
to feel pride, whether king or field mouse.
Before this evening, you will know the
magnitude of the smallest."

Shlomo listened to the queen's words and understood that they were just and wise. He bent over and decided that he would never again allow himself to be carried away by arrogance.

A little later, as the creatures were rushing to greet him, he noticed a young insect apart from the rest, busying himself in a hole.

"Why are you working, boy ant, whereas everyone else is celebrating and coming to see me?"

"Majesty, I would have indeed greeted you but I am engaged in an activity that is dear to me—I want to move this sand dune!"

"Poor boy ant," retorted the king with a laugh, "I doubt if you have the necessary strength, patience, and longevity to accomplish this wonder."

"Sometimes I doubt it too," confessed the boy ant, "but what I am certain of is the incredible strength that enlivens me, more powerful than the tempest, more impetuous than 'the tongues of the lashing sand'; I'm speaking to you about the power of love. On the other side of the dune my beloved lives and breathes. If I gave up my quest to join her, I would end this life in madness, deprived of this waterfall that streams into the heart of beings, which is hope."

Before the evening arrived, Shlomo had known the magnitude of the smallest and he was overwhelmed by the power of love. He thought about this power that saturated the air, contemplated the beauty of nature, and felt the poetic tide rising in him, which foreshadowed his Song of Songs.* *Stay me with flagons, comfort me with apples, for I am sick of love . . .*

Shlomo talked with the trees, the water, the flowers, and the stones in this way. He drew from them the tenderness necessary to ripen his fruits of wisdom. He understood that the letters forming all things were the words of love of the Nameless, *Shir Hashirim*, this Song of Songs is the heart of being.

* *The Canticle of Canticles.*

A Pearl
Is a Pearl

S hlomo Hamelech, son of David and king
of Israel, was the most enlightened of
men. His judgments restored the channels
damaged by the place the light falls, unifying
righteousness and goodness.

His beloved daughter, Ketsia, had been
raised in the temple of Jerusalem and she
had a unique beauty. Add a quick mind and
unequaled wisdom and you have an idea of
the music emanating from her person. It
was as if King David, her grandfather, had
handed down the charm of his harp and
his song to her. When she was a young,
accomplished girl, King Solomon thought
about her marriage. He consulted the stars
and the High Priest, who questioned his
breastplate studded with twelve stones:
Ketsia's qualities and virtues obliged her
to marry the pearl of the sons of Israel.

The most High's reply left King Solomon
puzzled: *An impoverished young man,
perhaps the poorest of the kingdom,* would
marry her. He envisioned taking Ketsia
away from Jerusalem and building a high
tower with no stairway on the open ocean.
He chartered a vessel to carry a cargo of
stones, and sent fifty zealous servants to
build the tower on an island in secret, and
to surround it with thick walls.

"If this is the Lord's will, His word will
be done. Wherever it happens to be, a pearl
is a pearl."

Three months passed and the tower was
ready. A cozy room with basic furniture at
the top of the turret awaited the princess.
The servants returned unobtrusively,
gave account, and waited. King Solomon
summoned his daughter one morning
and told her to prepare for a journey of
uncertain duration, the destination of
which he was keeping secret. He was
astonished that she was in a good mood,
and that his news of a sudden departure
did not sadden her. He added that she

would be alone and would live in a very modest place.

"All my life," she replied, "I have waited for this tender moment, to obey my father like the bird who knows nothing of flight and opens its wings trustingly. I imagine that your reason is woven with love and wisdom."

He smiled.

"And so you are not afraid?"

"Isn't the person who is fulfilled in love greater than the person who achieves something in a state of fear?"

"Indeed."

The king ordered his servants to leave with his daughter. They embarked, dropped Ketsia off in her retreat, and returned to the palace. King Solomon, commander of the birds, summoned the eagle with large wings that had carried him away years earlier to the desert of Tadmor, and asked him to bring hot meals prepared in the palace kitchens to the princess every day.

The hourglass had scarcely started trickling the sand through its chambers

when, a long way from the island and
Jerusalem, a young man called Reuven
was walking naked, alone, and starving
in the forest. Shivering with cold, he was
desperately looking for a spring. He saw
the warm carcass of a bull in the center of
the road and he nestled in its flank as if in
a bed and fell asleep. At midnight, the white
eagle flew overhead, making its way toward
the ocean with warm rolls for the princess.
He spotted the carcass, which looked like
the shape of the letter aleph on the ground,
and carried it away into the sky. When he
arrived at the top of the tower, he deposited
the rolls. He feasted on a portion of meat on
the roof and then went back to Jerusalem. At
dawn, the young girl came out of her cozy
room to contemplate the sunrise and was
astounded to see the bull carcass. As she
drew near, wondering about this marvel, she
saw a young man sleeping, huddled between
its flanks. Her soft voice woke Reuven and
he looked with astonishment at the height of
the place, the carcass located up there, and the
graceful young girl who was addressing him.

"Who are you?"

"I am a destitute Jew and I'm cold. I warmed myself up in this poor beast and I really don't know how I got here."

"For some secret reason, the eagle carried you away."

She took pity on his appearance, led him to her room, and offered him the golden rolls, which were still warm. Even though he was starving, first he wanted to thank the Lord by uttering a short prayer. She helped him wash, offered him some clean clothes and saw how handsome and bright he was, curious about cerebral matters, and yet endowed with a hearty, infectious, and clear laugh.

"The only problem is the sky, as there's no stairway. We're confined together until my father's servants return."

The next day, the eagle brought a hot meal for Ketsia and noticed Reuven.

Therefore, in the following days he doubled the rations. The young girl quickly fell in love with the man who had come to her from the sky. Filled with joy, he ventured to snuggle with her. They became husband and wife and were blessed by the most High. The months passed, punctuated by the coming and going of the eagle, until the day when Ketsia gave birth to a child and the bird brought an extra little meal.

During these times, one evening King Solomon questioned the eagle, who replied:

"Your daughter, Master, her young husband, and their little boy are doing well."

"It was the Lord's will. His word is done. Wherever it happened to be, the pearl was the pearl."

King Solomon agreed to go and welcome this hallowed island. The king led his entire assembly on an expedition and he climbed right to the top of the tower on a large ladder, squeezed his daughter tightly around her heart, and discovered the husband chosen by the sky, and the child. Love was the friend of these three and the king rejoiced.

The Leaf of Life

A papyrus professes that in the middle of the desert, a Berber Jew was suddenly illuminated by a leaf from the Tree of Life. I have picked up his trail and pieced together his story.

In North Africa and the Middle East, the story of Abergel is recounted, this well-known, miserly merchant, with his infamous and shapeless leather slippers clinging to his feet. Time and time again, I have heard my companions, the Arab storytellers, cheering while gradually destroying his avid deceit, until on examination he becomes a wandering, wise, and tattered king. Each has their own version and I can't resist the pleasure of telling you mine, acquired partly by a storyteller from the city of Fez who had traveled from Cordoba (who obtained it from an enlightened storyteller from Baghdad), and partly from the secrets of

the famous tale itself coming and going
between my lips as it pleases, changing its
nature for the love of fellow beings; not to
mention the dream I had one day on the
road to Jerusalem, and which whispered
the end of the tale to me.

There was once a well-known miserly
merchant who pleaded poverty; he was
also greedy and roguish. He had no qualms
about begging for a meal from poor people,
who were Jews like himself, but they had
open hearts and simple souls. On that day
in the market, he did what the giants do
when they see a wretched person on the
ground—he took advantage of a merchant's
failure and for a small pittance raided his
entire market stall of flasks of rose oil.

As he was humming a melody and
making the purse hidden in his pocket jangle,
he came up with the idea to celebrate his
great acquisition at the hammam. He could
no longer remember the words of the melody,
but the tune was still there, hiding away
like destiny, which whispered incognito:
Al más fuerte hombre, tapa la tierra,—even

the strongest man is one day covered by the earth. Thus, he entered the Moorish bath, undressed in the communal changing room, and put his filthy leather slippers next to dozens of richly colored mules.

After he had chuckled with happiness in the hot water, washed, shaved, groomed, and anointed himself with perfume, Abergel the miser went to get dressed. But imagine his surprise when he saw that in the place he thought he had put his worn-out old slippers was an interlaced pair of slippers, embroidered and set with two rubies. His business that morning must have been carried to a very lofty place: The Lord had sent one of his angels to give him this gift! *You, who can transform the rock into a lake, You have turned my poor soles into flowers . . .* Whosoever speaks with his God without a mediator, but only talks with his shadow, is close to madness: Abergel put on the magnificent slippers and left blissfully happy.

Rapture was not the sentiment that came over the judge of the rabbinical court when he noticed Abergel's famous

slippers in place of his own. Abergel was
summoned on the spot, convicted of theft,
and given a heavy fine equivalent to twice
the price of the goods in the market stall
belonging to the bankrupt tradesman. In
a raging temper, having given the slippers
back to their rightful owner and retrieved
his own, he threw them into the stream
and returned barefoot. The slippers
floated like little boats until they came up
against the net of a fisherman. The judge's
slippers were famous, while Abergel's
wrath was notorious. The man ran into
the town with his catch, and aimed at the
scoundrel's window, who at that moment
was pouring the last flask of rose oil into
his large crystal decanter. He had just
put the stopper down when the slippers
hurtled into the room, bursting the flasks
open and smashing the decanter, whose
precious liquid trickled onto the ground.

Al más fuerte hombre . . . Even the most
prosperous of men yanks the hairs out of
his goatee beard when his fortune goes up
in smoke. He went out, dug a hole in his

garden, and buried the accursed slippers. A passing dog dug them up and brought them back to the judge, whose scent he had sniffed on the slippers. What an insult! Another huge fine was in order.

Now even more enraged, Abergel came out of the court with his slippers and threw them into the distance, into the reservoir of rainwater serving the city. They floated for a moment and then drifted up to the conduit supplying the large hammam, and clogged it. Men were told to dive in, the disruption was recognized, and the foolhardy Abergel was pronounced guilty. It had only taken two days to ruin Abergel. All he was left with was his house.

Al más fuerte hombre . . . the little tune ran through his head; he had no wish to sing but searched for the words buried in his memory. He felt something staring at him: the eyes of his slippers. When he had brought his slippers into the house the day before, he had thrown them out of the window at the very moment the rabbi's wife had been passing. She had jumped out of the way, fallen on the pavement, cut her lips, and broken an arm and a tooth.

"Your house is seized," said the judge as he gave Abergel his slippers back.

"Thank you," replied the unfortunate man while laughing. And unexpected, great sorrows that had been buried came into this world as a result of these peals of laughter. When he crossed the cedar forest, he hung his slippers on a tree. He was laughing, shaken, and chuckling at himself, while cursing his gloomy fate. He stopped in front of the desert, barefoot in the sand. The words of the melody came back to him: *Al más fuerte hombre, tapa la tierra,—even the strongest man is one day covered by the earth.* He laughed again.

I would like to be Djohaya the rebel, Djoha's sister, in order to describe him and to encourage you to follow him and hear the end of this tale, which came to me in Jerusalem.

He walked like this over days, nights, and months, barefoot on the sacred earth. One evening, he noticed a bright star in a zone the astrologers called The Stable, and followed it until he could see it licking the dunes. He entered the light, and saw an infant in a straw basket, his mother, his father, and some shepherds. They made room for him and he went to greet the child, who was speaking the language of the birds. Abergel took his hand with a gentle laugh. The child thanked him with a smile and, in a language that only the ox and the donkey surrounding him understood, Abergel chanted: *The place where repentant sinners reside, the perfect righteous cannot reside.*

Abergel went on his way at a leisurely pace, and walked on a leaf from the Tree of Life, which became his own skin.

The Powder-
Maker's Choice

So King Poziol was dead. As he was the
last of a long line, it left the Polish throne
desperately vacant. The nobility had held a
council in great haste, as they had to elect
a new monarch. But where could they find
this rare bird? The candidates for the throne
didn't even have the makings of a minor king
of the provinces; they had to unearth a king
quickly, mutually agree on his name, and
elect him for there to be legitimacy. They
debated for hours in this way, and were so
weary and short of ideas that they endorsed
the opinion of the Grand Master of their
assembly: the first man who passed through
the gates of Kruszwica at dawn would be their
ruler! The outskirts of the birthplace of the
former dynasty, on the shores of Lake Goplo,
were dotted with sentries and its bridges
and gates were patrolled by watchmen. At

dawn, they noticed a man entering the city. It was the famous powder-maker, Abraham Prochownik! The watchmen greeted him by cheering and surrounding him, entreating him to follow them hastily. He was staggered by their manner. He had never heard of such an amicable arrest. It is indeed rare that a man surrounded by soldiers could imagine that he has become king. Dubiously, he presented himself before the electoral college of nobles and was astonished when one of the judges bowed to him. The watchmen confirmed that this man was undeniably the first to have crossed the boundary of Kruszwica at the same time as the sun crossed the horizon. The Grand Master spoke and thanked providence for its choice. He explained to the powder-maker the reason for his presence, praised the honest and gifted artist who knew all the secrets of powder, and who, having brightened up the faces of the kingdom, would be entrusted with the soul of a people.

Abraham was a simple and modest man—wasn't his trade about enabling others to combine a little magic with their

desire to be noticed? And unobtrusiveness suited him well. He cleared his throat, bowed his head to seek forgiveness, and said:

"Gentlemen, you entrust your lot to destiny and you approve of its choice with a great deal of dignity and affection, but would you have forgotten that I am a Jew?"

"No," replied the Grand Master, "but we have set out the terms of succession; we accept its rules, and our prince is elected, even if he's a Jew. You entered with the dawn like the king we were waiting for." Those present applauded, and their hats

and cheering soared; and the bells rang out *Long live Abraham!* The powder-maker knew that he was valued for his advice on make-up and grooming; he had always been treated well by the nobility, but ennobling him and proclaiming him prince, with him being a poor Jew, was another matter and seemed utter madness. When silence reigned again, he continued:

"Polish people, everything has gone very fast. Give yourselves and me a day of reflection, talk among yourselves, and assess the benefits and risks of how it befits people of noble status. As for me, I must seek the help of my God within the silence of meditation. Allow me to retreat to my humble abode and, if you please, do not come and disturb this time of truth.

So they waited until the new monarch had finished conversing with his God. But once the time limit had passed, they began to worry and pace in circles. The nobles took turns in the courtroom for long hours over a period of two more days. Abraham remained alone in his little abode on the shores of the lake. Nobody dared interrupt him—can one disturb a king? The crowd became impatient, and the courtesans were fainting, as they had been confined in their corsets for hours and the effects of the powder they had plastered on their faces were turning into a nightmare. Then, one of the nobles of great stature, named Piast, spoke and harangued the crowd:

"Since nobody here has the courage to bring this waiting to an end, and as our land cannot remain without a leader, I

shall go and fetch our sovereign, whatever it costs me." The man strode off, followed by the nobility and the whole assembly. Three days had passed and the powder-maker king prayed fervently to the Lord to whisper the words of deliverance to him.

"Abraham Prochownik, prince of Poland, in the name of the people, what does the truth say?"

The door opened and the powder-maker came forward, with his hands clasped.

"The truth says that I am sorry to have made you languish but it also thinks that this wait was beneficial. You see, it's already difficult enough to govern yourself, to apply powder to people's faces with artistry. Not with a view to concealing their faces, oh not that, but so that they take pleasure in their true colors when they're preparing for a romantic encounter. When I put on a touch of paint to reveal their being—that is when I am king. I've heard the voice of a real leader among you—the man who has just summoned me, a man who is ready to serve you and doesn't tremble. Take him, put a crown on his head; this is the only serious step you can take."

A long silence greeted the truth. The powder-maker, without practicing his art, had just ennobled a thousand faces in search of enlightenment.

"Hurrah," the people shouted, "long live Piast, our leader!"

The prince's rule was favorable to the Jews, and it didn't forget the wisdom and the art of the powder-maker, Abraham Prochownik.

The Language
of the Kings

I t was snowing along the Vistula River
and a Jew was washing his clothes on a
partially covered stone. The emperor was
passing at that moment with his retinue and
noticed the man scrubbing the fabric in the
icy water. He guided his horse as far as the
bank and asked him:

"Tell me, what is more for you, five or
seven?"

And the Jew raised his head and
replied, unconcerned:

"I say, what is more for me, twelve or
thirty-two?"

The emperor nodded and added:

"Has your house ever caught fire?"

"As a matter of fact, it has already
caught fire five times and I'm anticipating
two more fires."

"If I send you one of my pigeons, will
you know how to pluck it correctly?"

"Send it to me; you will not be disappointed."

The riders in the procession were listening but didn't understand anything. When they were on the cobbles, the emperor leaned toward his palatine and said to him:

"Viceroy, *you* are my legatee, did you understand the eloquent conversation we engaged in, this Jew and I?"

"I ... er ... admired the covert language of Your Majesty, the excellent method, but it was so brief and in truth ... "

"You should be ashamed. This poor Jew understood everything and he speaks the coded language of the emperor. You have three days to unravel this mystery. If you go beyond this time limit, you will be honored by your reply or revoked through your ignorance."

The palatine nearly failed in his task. The day had started well and it was turning into a nightmare. The snowfall that had seemed light to him was now getting in his eyes and blinding him. When he got back to the palace, he sent for the Jew and asked

him to translate the dialogue he had with the emperor.

"No, if you had asked me to wash a shirt for you, then that would have cost you a few zlotys. But to translate the language of the poor and the kings is a luxury that can only be offered to those who pay with a purse full of gold. Reflect on this."

The viceroy racked his brains for two days and went off to take the purse himself to the Jew.

"Well?"

"The emperor saw me washing my rags in the icy water. Then he asked me if the seven hot months of the year seemed longer to me than the five months of wintry weather. Namely, was I able to set a little aside in summer to sustain me through the winter. I said to him: 'What is more for me, twelve or thirty-two?' By this I wanted to convey to him that my thirty-two teeth required more than I could set aside for them in twelve months. Afterward, he asked me if my house had ever caught fire. I said that it has already caught fire five times, because of the five children that I have already married off. After that, you get through it somehow, as you do in the wake of a great fire. I added that I was anticipating two more fires—you see, I have two daughters left at the house and a respectable dowry is like a flame licking the walls."

"And the pigeon that he suggested you pluck," continued the viceroy, afraid of forgetting part of the riddle.

"I told him to send it to me and that I would pluck it for him. It is now for you to find out, to check with the emperor that I have done it appropriately."

וַיְהִי בְּשַׁלַּח פַּרְעֹה

בַּעֲלֵה קַמְלָה מוּרֵל מֵאֵפֶס בּוֹרֵא בַּעֲשׂוֹת בַּעֲלֵי יִשְׂרָאֵל וַיָּבוֹא
וַיִּשְׁמֹר מִמְּעֹנֵי וַיֵּלֶךְ מִנְגַּח נֶצַח
מִיַּד יוֹשֵׁב בּוֹרֵא מַלְכֵּי בַּעֲלֵי שַׁרְבִי
בְּיַד מַלְאֲכֵי בַּעֲלֵי מֵיַד שָׁרַי
וְיֹשֵׁב מְעֹרֵל מֵאֵל בּוֹרֵא

אֲשֶׁר יוֹרֵל קַמְלָה שַׁעֲשֵׁל יֹשְׁמֵעַ
אַחֲרֵי בַּעֲשׂוֹת מֵעֹרֵל נֶצַח

וַיֹּאמֶר

The Love Doctor

*Hold out your hands and choose your
destiny, but don't expect the Holy Name
to spare you the duty of achieving it.*
Marek Halter, *The Kabbalist of Prague*

Rabbi Moshe ben Maimon, called Mussa
bin Maimun ibn Abdallah al-Kurtubi
al-Israili by Muslims, better known as
Maimonides or Rambam, was an eminent
medieval sage, a philosopher, and a famous
doctor of the Arab-Andalusian and the Judeo-
Muslim golden age. Born in Cordoba, and
forced to flee persecution, he passed through
Granada, Seville, Almería, Fez, and Palestine
before he reached Egypt. This prominent
humanist, who descended from the line of
David, wrote books and treatises. The course
of his journey left behind a delightful trail of
stories, in which he is both *the Prince of doctors*
and *the Eagle of the Synagogue*.

It is said that his father had the same dream several times. A venerable man with a white beard had appeared to him, telling him to make his way to Cordoba and to take the daughter of a certain butcher for his wife. A son would be born from their union, a wise man whose light would illuminate Israel and the world. Although disturbed by this, the Andalusian obeyed his vision; he proposed and married the young girl. A year later, she gave birth to Moshe. Thus began the destiny of the man who would go on to write numerous books of wisdom, give counsel, protect the Jews, and with great dignity look after all those who would have need of it, whether rich or poor, Jews or Arabs. But like all those who excel, tend, and engage in this world, he aroused jealousy and meanness.

The sultan heard about Maimonides's medical knowledge and, as his own doctor had just died, he suggested to the wise man that he succeed him. This news made the Egyptian scholars livid. When they learned that he had accepted the position, their anger and resentment poured out. The sultan had preferred a Jew to them, a foreigner who made no distinction between a prince and a beggar, and who dared to recite his medical Prayer: *My God, grant that I may see but the man in the sufferer. . . . Sustain the strength of my heart so that it is always ready to serve the poor man and the rich man, the friend and the enemy, the good and the bad . . . drive the quacks away from their beds.*

War was declared as far as these jealous doctors were concerned, and they would resort to any means to bring about the downfall of this interloper—a madman who asked his God to make him invulnerable to mockery. As was customary at that time, a learned assembly resided in the sultan's court and would adjudicate on every occasion. Shortly after Maimonides's appointment, they instigated a dispute on the subject of blindness. In contrast to the doctor, they maintained that the sight of a man born blind could be restored. As they were anticipating, Moshe ben Maimon didn't change his mind, even though he was facing a mob. He dared to stand up to the councilors, who appealed to the judgment of the sultan. A blind man was brought in and introduced as being deprived of light from birth. One of them came forward holding a bowl of an oily, fragrant ointment, anointed his eyelids with it and asked the blind man to blink his eyes several times. He waited and backed away a step in a theatrical way. An exclamation of joy gushed forth from the man, who bobbed up and down as he thanked the erudite magicians profusely. The sultan had inclined his head slightly, which indicated that a suggestion of incompetence insinuated by the scholars had hit home. Maimonides approached the man who was miraculously healed and said to him in a gentle voice:

"My good man, what am I holding in my hand?"

"A handkerchief, it's completely red too," added the healed man for good measure.

"This ointment is magic, I readily admit, and it will have taught this man, who was

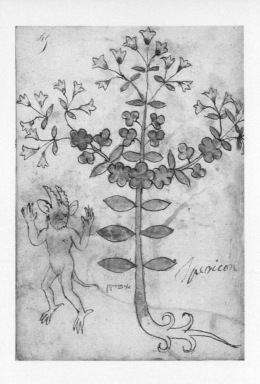

born blind, the names of the colors quicker than a newborn introduced to light."

The sultan seemed to wake up all of a sudden, hit his chair with his fist and saluted the wisdom of his doctor.

"We have the opportunity to have you by our side. Not only are you a scholar, but you possess the qualities of King Solomon and have his bearing. Let the mockers get out of my sight for a whole phase of the moon!"

The incident strengthened the hatred of the cheats. Thirty days later, they pleaded with the sovereign to receive a man called Kamoun, an unequaled doctor of Egyptian blood, and alone worthy of watching over the sultan's precious health. When they saw that the sultan had not decided, they played a clever game, adding fuel to the fire, calling for a battle of wits between Kamoun and the Jew, promising that at the end of this confrontation no one would further call into question the legitimacy of the victor, whoever he might be.

The sultan found the offer attractive and radical. Since all these people seemed to like spice, he was going to give them some! He summoned the two doctors, telling them he would only entrust his own life to the most powerful scholar of his generation.

"Since nature has entrusted you with the preparations that save or kill and your knowledge of remedies takes into account the science of dosages and concoctions, may the best doctor poison the other and protect himself from the deadly toxins of his adversary. The skill of the man who emerges victorious from the war will be indisputable and will no longer be able to be questioned, without warranting punishment."

Kamoun unleashed a ferocious smile. Experienced, cunning, and the perpetrator of a large number of poisonings ordered by high-ranking people, his notion of his profession conflicted with how Maimonides viewed it. That a doctor could be capable of compromising himself by formulating a poison was bewildering to Maimonides, even if it were to triumph in an insane battle of wits. However, he agreed, telling himself that he would indeed find a solution to this thorny problem. He had no intention of letting himself be killed, any more than he would make an attempt on the life of others.

The only answer was to anticipate the onslaught and assemble the ingredients and daring counterattacks in his laboratory. One evening, he suffered pain after he had eaten a cake, the contents of which he identified; he swallowed the antidote and emerged the next day as fresh as a daisy in the presence of the sultan and his poisoner. Kamoun had himself poured in the deadly poison . . . anxiety changed sides. What could this Jew have prepared that was capable of outsmarting the poison? Which poison was he going to concoct for him?

"Be very careful and surround yourself with panaceas," said Maimonides ardently, "I have something for you. It's scrumptious, fellow doctor."

While Kamoun did his utmost to pour out his deadly flasks, in order to make an attempt on Maimonides's life, he swallowed the assortment of antidotes, which played havoc with his stomach and intestines, and he poisoned himself. Maimonides was calmer. The worst creations of the Egyptian always revolved around the same basic ingredients; his rage made him double and triple the dosages, making them more easily corrected and curiously less toxic. Kamoun could not suppose for one moment that Maimonides was not trying to kill him. He convinced himself he must have absorbed one of these African plants, the effects of which come later. He redoubled his arsenal of devastating antidotes. He nourished himself solely with the milk from a goat that he milked himself and wandered in the corridors of the palace with his jug and accompanied by his fear. When he thought the Jew had poisoned the goat, he rolled to the floor, seized by convulsions, and died.

The sultan rushed up, accompanied by his retinue of scholars. They felt the goat's weight, and they sniffed it. Everyone made their own conjectures as regards the poison used, but Maimonides merely nodded. He had a child brought over, gave it the milk to drink, and when it had wiped its lips with relish, everyone understood that it was not the poison that had killed Kamoun.

"Your Lordship," an occultist said to the sultan, "You had authorized the poison; the Jew has entered into an agreement with the powers of darkness. This sorcerer deserves to die!"

Lapis Sophorum

Maimonides smiled and as he lifted the palm of his hand, said:

"That which is within you, do not let it govern you; there is nothing here that smacks of sorcery. Kamoun died of fear. He has dug a pit and has made it deep; he has slid into the pit that he had prepared. I am a doctor, not a poisoner. I have contented myself with evasion, and that is for the good; whosoever is in charge of a pious task will know no harm."

The sultan asked him to tell the story of the past weeks and Maimonides spoke. His voice was the voice of truth and everyone believed him; everyone held him in high esteem. He admitted that the ordeal had been harsh but also fruitful, since it had enriched his knowledge and he had found new remedies. He accepted the position of doctor to the sultan, welcomed the contrition of the scholars, and forgave them.

The Harvest of Songs

After one of the maassiot, or remedy tales, by
Rabbi Nahman of Bratslav.

We have seen the legend flow, from
the mouth of the Rebbe, from his
eyes filled with intangible joy. He narrated
as he nodded his head, "honey and milk were
under his tongue,"* on his whiskers and his
beard. He was inviting us to listen to the song
of the flowers, to surrender ourselves to the
confidences of the Tree of Life, to open ourselves up and be creative for the meaning to
be renewed. There were treasures concealed
in his language, and his tongue became supple
so that the hidden face of the words might be
perceived. He told the story unassumingly,
letting the sorrow well up and inviting it to
join us, in order to spring into a state of elation.

I remember the evening when he brought us together, assuming the voice of one of the seven beggars who was traveling the world to harvest, he said, all the noble deeds, and take them to a weaver able to gather together the song of the creatures, by weaving long enough for life and love to perpetuate.

"I have seen it there where I have seen it. There was a mountain and on the mountain a stone. A spring was gushing forth from this stone. Here, there, and everywhere, each object possesses a heart: bread, the olive, the child, the world too. And the heart of the world has its own body and looks well; the nail on its foot contains the essence of the heart, more than any other heart. Thus at one end of the world the stone and the mountain were situated, where the spring was gushing forth. The heart of the world lived at the other end, facing it. When the heart saw the spring, his desire was aroused and he uttered a protracted cry: he wanted to get nearer to his beloved. His lassitude and this desire were infinite. While he was crying out, praying for the will to reach

her, and while she, herself, passionately desired this heart, he was suffering from two afflictions. Burned by the heat of the sun and with a raging thirst, he was gripped by a longing for their union. He continued to walk, still on the other side, overcome, yearning, with his chest inflamed with his desire. Sometimes, he had to rest and build his strength. Then a bird came and spread its wings to protect him from the scorching rays of the sun. Under the shelter of its wings, he regained his strength. But faced with a longing for his beloved, his unfathomable sorrow still drove him to continue. As soon as he approached, a shadow was cast on the heart; petrified, he could no longer see either the summit or the spring up there. He was going to die, he and the world with him, alongside all the creatures with a heart keeping everything alive. Therefore, he went back from where he had started and began everything again—the cry, the desire, the thirst. . . . He had to yield and get back to the place from where his eyes drew their strength, from where he kept the world alive.

He could not take his eyes off the spring
without it disappearing too.

"Thus, the heart of the world remained
at the other end, guessing that it was going
to love without ever embracing, but would
merely caress its eyes, the blue gold of
eternity. The sun had rejoined the heart
of the world and was distilling time. Soon
night was going to fall and the heart of the
world would no longer see the spring. It
would die as a result of this and alongside

all creatures with a heart. The spring that was oblivious of the days and the flow of time, and lived much higher than time, would disappear from the world."

At this point in the story, our Rebbe beggar stopped; he clapped his hands and continued in a cheerful tone, and all of a sudden they knew that he was both a big kid and a notable wise man, passionate about his frantic and luxuriant faith.

"The heart of the world has sung, the spring has replied and the two voices have united in space, combined so as to create no more than a song, sprinkled into every creature. Each creature hears it, and understands it in its own way. The heart of the world is on the point of dying and the spring will disappear."

The Rebbe, with his eyes twinkling mischievously, held up his finger inquiringly toward our mournful foreheads.

"Who wants to give his song to the weaver and add it to the songs of the bread, the olive, and the child, so that he will gather them all together and weave some time?"

Nobody hesitated. We all wanted to offer another day to the heart of the world. Rabbi Nahman *zatsal* harvested our fervent songs, and delicately collected the gifts in his hands and threw them joyously like sparks:

"My children, you have offered your songs, this additional day in the heart of the world that in turn offers it to the spring, while singing. Nothing is going to die here, there, or anywhere. You are forbidden to be old! Become the voice of love; rejoice in the harvest because each man is a letter. Your power is to gather that which does not disappear!"

Playfully, he combined the tones of the beggar in the story with his own voice again.

He laughed as he wiped the honey and the milk from his tongue. Then he invited us to dance.

* *The Canticle of Canticles* IV, 11.

Soup from the Garden of Eden

Lying in his bed, Rabbi Elimelech was gradually taking leave of the earth. Just as the saints who depart, he was calm and without any desire for this world. His son was hoping that he would taste the flavors of his cooking again and so offered him a small, delicate, and golden *kuchen*.

"Father, are you no longer partial to fresh nuts or orange blossom? Have you lost your appetite, because you've left my bread that I flavored with violet seeds? Would you like me to make you an apple strudel?"

Smiling, the old man replied:

"No thank you, son, but you have whetted the appetite of my mind. The unequalled taste of a memory is coming back to me, and that's enough for me since I barely have the time to get there, where

my palace, long ago, started to sing. Sit
down and listen as if we were invited into
the kitchen of King David or were guests
around King Solomon's table.

"One day we were traveling by road
to Gdansk with the gentle Rabbi Zusya.
We were starving and it was late when we
found a poor, completely dilapidated inn.
And here, a woman served us a noodle soup
that nevertheless would make me laugh
and cry. I would like to taste this soup if
the Lord of weavers gave me another day
to do so. But you see, it's too late, I chew
on my last memory with a gratified heart."

With these words, Rabbi Elimelech
took his last breath. After he had finished
crying and had buried his father, Rabbi
Eleazar desired to go on a pilgrimage on
the road to Gdansk, in order to find the
dilapidated inn and its cook, if she was
living and still working in that premises. In
the evening, he saw the inexpensive eating-
house and went in. A woman undefeated
by age welcomed him; she had disheveled
hair. There was a table near the fire where

three places were laid. It seemed to him that he was sitting with the two Servants of God who had preceded him here.

"I'm very hungry, and I'm tired," he said.

"I have almost nothing set aside," replied the cook, "I just have a simple noodle soup to offer you."

She was unaware how much her single dish surpassed the promise of a *klops* or a *cholent* in the eyes of the Rabbi.

"A noodle soup? That will be ideal." he replied.

The cook, who was reassured by his reply, disappeared into the kitchen. Rabbi Eleazar contented himself with a short prayer followed by a long silence: *"Blessed art Thou, Lord our God, King of creation, blessed be this festive soup, this kind-hearted woman and the rare herbs that she's preparing. Amen . . ."*

He had scarcely finished his meditation when the cook returned with her tureen. He took the chipped soup-ladle, which was very probably the same one his father and Rabbi Zusya had used to fill their bowls, and tasted the soup. Adonai, what a masterpiece! He wiped his bowl clean, had a second helping, asked for a third, and ate like three starving Rabbis, not through greed but out of respect for loved ones, and he tried to solve the mystery of the basic flavors that made up the soup.

"Woman, did you bring back the fruits from the Garden of Eden to achieve this divine flavor?"

"Upon my word, sir, first and foremost I added a few noodles to water!"

And when Eleazar looked at her wide-eyed and incredulous, she told him:

"Long ago, one evening, two starving Servants of God came to me here. I was just as I stand before you, as deprived of nutritious greenery as a bare tree. I only had some noodles and fresh water to make a soup and I also prayed to God to give it some flavor. 'Oh Adonai,' I whispered, 'I have absolutely nothing, neither orange tuber, nor garlic, nor cabbage, nor oil, and you whose words are woven from nature, you whose breath is so sublime, you are almighty. Have pity on these two Servants of God, worn out by the long distance they have traveled. Go into your Garden of Eden and choose two or three fine spices, invite a few large festive turnips, some joyous potatoes, and oh, if you please, let this soup refresh their bodies and enlighten their minds.' They must have liked my soup from heaven, as they ate two tureens of it! One of them said: 'Thank you for your soup, flavored with the herbs of Paradise!' This was undoubtedly sincere because eyes like those do not lie. When I saw you today, Rabbi, I remembered the recipe."

"Oh she is worthy of King David's kitchen and King Solomon's table," Eleazar mused with a smile. Delighted, he thought about his father, the tzadik, who liked putting stars between words. The cook was one of these modest people who possess something unique and whose wisdom is derived more from unrest than from study. It seemed to him that Elimelech and Zusya would have liked him to accompany this thought with dancing.

The Wise Man's Judgment

When Torquemada presided over the tribunals of the Spanish Inquisition, he hounded all those he marked out as "infidels." He wanted to drive out the Moors from Spain, he pursued the Jews and Muslims who had converted to Catholicism, and summoned the unyielding to leave the country. Contact with Christians was forbidden, people had to convert to Catholicism against their will, and the Talmud was burned, forcing a multitude of Jews into exile.

There is a story of a rabbi, a contemporary of Isaac Abravanel, indicted by the representatives of the local Inquisition, who were entrusted with confiscating the property of the heretics, trying, and torturing them. Firstly, the accused man was brought in before his judges. Moreover, the inquisitor, with caustic humor, suggested

by way of an exceptional measure to wager
the death of this Jew rather than subject him
to "the question."

"Understand that I set before you the
judgment of God. I am writing *innocent*
on this slip and *guilty* on the other one. All
you have to do is select one at random from
this box. If God wills it, you will leave here
a free man and be exonerated by the Holy
Office of the Inquisition, or you will be put
to death."

"I marvel at your clemency. Don't the
poor wretches unjustly accused of heresy
have their bones crushed or stomachs
submerged first, and this prior to the
Holy Office of the Inquisition delivering a
judgment as to their guilt?"

"Clemency sometimes accompanies the
rules of divine justice. Do not complain
about benefiting from it. If you are
innocent, you have nothing to fear from it."

The accused man withstood the cold
and lugubrious face of his interlocutor and
thought that he was unlikely to embrace
his fellow man often or know how to laugh

at himself. The man was known for his hatred of Jews, irrespective of whether an artisan, tradesman, or rabbi, man, woman, or child. He was convinced of his duplicity, certain that the cheat had written *guilty* on both slips. He felt pity for the Christian God who didn't deserve a representative like this one on earth and shuddered in the face of so much impiety. However, he stretched out his hand unfalteringly and took out one of the two slips without trembling and swallowed it before anyone could stop him.

"What have you done, you are now convicted. How can I judge you, if you have swallowed God's reply?" the judge shouted.

"God's reply rests in the hand of the inquisitor. By revealing to the public the sentence that was not intended for me, it will be easy to read the one I accept and digest."

All eyes turned toward the inquisitor, who had to, as it were, comply.

Complete, Is
What We Are!

The *tzadik* Rabbi Zusya said that the man who demonstrates he is bold and adventurous enough to venture onto the path of holiness is authorized to descend into Hell in order to discover what's down there. The bold man can run down the streets, frequent the fairs, even rub shoulders with the abyss without fear of the Evil One. Foolish and wise, Rabbi Zusya dedicated his life to the awakening of souls. He used the familiar form of address to the Lord, wandered through Poland, liberated prisoners and birds, and spoke gently to the earth.

In the twilight of his long life, as he was dying amid his disciples, he started to cry. Creating a circle of love around the master, his pupils talked in loud voices of what he had been for them.

"Rabbi," they lamented. "What will become of us, have you not been our Moses and this abode our Mount Sinai?"

As he looked disconsolate, they developed the metaphors pertaining to Moses, recalling the Land of Canaan where he had led them, and chanting prayers to the divine world where their Moses of Hanipol was going to ascend.

"Let us speak of it," said the wise man as he regained his full strength. "In this world to come, the question that I will be asked will not be: 'Tell me then, Zusya, why have you not been Moses?' No, the question I will be asked is the question the *Holy One, Blessed be he* will whisper to me in his lavishness, which is the only worthwhile one: 'Why have you not been yourself, Rabbi Zusya, from head to foot?'"

An Andalusian
Supper

I n the Al-Andalous, at the zenith of the
caliphate of Cordoba, just before the year
one thousand, the great civilizations were
forming a cultural mosaic. Peace and respect
were bringing a fruitful breath of fresh air, a
competitive spirit, and a blending of cultures.
The caliph, the benefactor, guaranteed the
coexistence of the communities, and watched
over the blossoming of a dynasty that did not
share the customs adopted by the Abbasids of
Baghdad. The Hispanics were able to convert
to Islam or remain Christians without being
subject to reprisals. The Jews took a very active
part in society, and the Talmudic school of
Cordoba was a hive of activity. The slaves who
had come from the Sudan and Europe were
able to become soldiers, and administrators,
and be liberated. This open-mindedness
affected those belonging to religious orders,

and they formed friendships and debated among themselves.

Thus a Mozarabic priest, a rabbi, and an imam were not only neighbors, but also good friends. They enjoyed teasing each other, and these cutting remarks that they would sometimes aim at each other were derived more from a jocular exploration of their differences than common animosity. In short, together they practiced the cult of humor, by laying themselves open to a battle of words and to the implacable test of self-mockery. Juggling between their obligations and the days devoted to worship, they found moments to exchange ideas, drink mint tea, and eat cakes. They established an annual celebration and took turns to welcome their brothers in their own way.

That year, it was the priest's turn. Considering his customary, mutinous wit, the rabbi and the imam were prepared for anything. He greeted them with a few words in *aljamía,* the strange Latin dialect of the Mozarabs, and said in Hebrew,

Arabic, and Castilian: "Welcome to your house." The tone was abrasive enough to arouse their suspicions: this meal would consist of honey and lemon. As he was serving the mint tea and the almond cakes, he broached the subject of the celebration and the mutual respect between the host and his guests.

"What is better than to delight the heart of a hungry man," said the imam, "The food you desire benefits you but the food you swallow without appetite devours you."

"A cooking pot had by several people is neither cold nor hot," commented the rabbi. "Let us honor the food *our father* has prepared for us."

The priest served up cold soup with onions and tomatoes. After he had tasted it and expressed his satisfaction, the rabbi said:

"We will do as we have been done by!"

"I would gladly have another helping now—the shroud has no pockets," the imam added, greedily.

"Let's move on to the wine," said the priest in a playful tone. "I can hear the footsteps of a loyal woman."

And he clapped his hands.

The imam frowned while the rabbi was delighted at this announcement, and then the servant arrived. She was old, frumpish, and quite unpleasant. The sight of the small crystal decanter and the bronze-colored wine eased the rabbi's disappointment, who greeted the precious nectar and the servant with these words:

"It's easier to appease a man than a woman."

The imam refused the wine, and pulling himself together, he flashed his broadest smile and cried out:

"If you seek a flawless brother, stay at home. I feel fine here."

Here we have the two complicit wine enthusiasts; they inhale, gurgle, and click their tongues.

"I did well to have another helping of soup."

"My dear imam," replied the rabbi, mockingly, "You don't know what you're missing!"

"Don't you preach in your sermons that whosoever is content with his lot in life, lacks nothing?"

"Yes, my friend and I like hearing you say that if the believer wishes for his brother what he wishes for himself, he only has his best interests at heart."

The servant returned with a pheasant.

This time, the priest and the imam were served and thoroughly enjoyed the pheasant. The rabbi refused the dish as it was impure to his palate. To console himself, he held out his glass for more wine and smiling said:

"How good it is to see these two children of God eating. Their happiness nourishes me."

When the two of them had finished licking their plates, the priest said to them:

"The man who knows how to be reprimanded is honored."

Then the unpleasant servant set a dish of piping-hot roast pork on the table. The Jew and the Muslim quickly calmed their agitation, before both feigning righteous anger.

"How can you do this to friends and insult them!"

"It's unworthy!"

And the priest ate his portion, contrite.

"Who is strong, Rabbi?" the imam asked the rabbi.

"The two guests, that is certain, who make a friend out of an enemy."

After the dish had been removed, they laughed heartily.

After the honey cakes and the infusion had arrived, the sparring stopped to give way to a simple discussion between brothers. They talked about the merest trifles of life, and about neighbors, and they told two funny stories; then it was time to leave.

"What a wonderful evening," said the imam. "Thanks again."

"Don't forget to say hallo to your wife," the rabbi added to the priest.

"But . . . ," the host said somewhat tipsily, "you're making fun of me. You know full well that I cannot have a wife!"

"Oh," said the imam and the rabbi in chorus. "What a pity, you don't know what you're missing!"

"The beauty of a woman is the intoxication of the heart," said the imam.

"But sometimes a man behaves like a pig," the rabbi said as he burst out laughing.

The signs of anger formed for a moment on the priest's forehead and eventually changed into resounding laughter.

"May you have a tender night, my brothers."

When the two guests found themselves beneath the stars, the imam placed his hand on the rabbi's shoulder:

"Are we too verbose, Kaleb?"

The rabbi smiled.

"The parlance of wise men is a soothing balm."

Two Stories About the Besht

"**M**aster, tell us a story!"

"It's an actual living thing, eh, my boy!"

It extends beyond the storyteller. It comes from a place where wounds and balms are known. A story told in such a way that it can, of its own accord, breathe life into dormant sorrows and elevate them. My grandfather was paralyzed, but he was a good storyteller. As he had had the opportunity of living close to the Baal Shem Tov, the storyteller knew a lot of legends through him. One day, gripped by a story, while describing the strange way in which the master was praying, he got up and danced around happily on the spot just as he had seen his grandfather do. The story had cured him! Come to think of it, among the legends brought back by the disciples of the Besht, two come to mind.

One day, the master remained alone in the house of prayer for several hours; the others had left. Later, he offered this story for purposes of contemplation because this solitude was detrimental.

"Wild geese flew over a distant country of the East. The indigenous people noticed an unparalleled bird with showy plumage in the center of these graceful creatures, flying like a poem offering itself up to the sky. The other geese surrounded it, while singing its praises. Nobody had ever observed a bird like this in living memory. As the geese alighted in the glade, it flew to the top of the highest tree and made its nest. When the king heard the news, he ordered it to be carefully taken down from the nest. He suggested that they create a human ladder running the entire length of the trunk, with each person climbing onto the shoulders of the next, and so forth. They would have to hold on tight and wait until the last person was at the height of the nest and would then come back down with the wonderful bird. It took some time to build this human chain. But those at the bottom couldn't stand it any longer—they fidgeted and down it came! Everything collapsed."

There are other prayer stories about the Besht, but I'm going to narrate something else for you. When Rabbi Yaakof Yossev was Rav of Sharigrod, he did not care for Hasidism. The movement was strict and it practiced mortification.

"One morning, a man arrived who no one knew; he alighted from his carriage right in the center of the market. Scarcely had he set his feet on the ground when he called a farmer over, who was dragging a cow behind him, and started telling him a story. Not only was the farmer struck by the tale, but the cow was transported by the story, the man's voice, and the images. All it took was for a passer-by to catch hold of a word and he was attached to the story like a piece of fruit to its cluster. The square soon turned into an enormous ear, and was both attentive and crowded. Moreover, the servant from the house of prayer was drawn in by the mellow turn of phrase and he sat down, open-mouthed, between two ducks. Despite the strictness of the rav, the punctual servant no longer had any notion of time. While one part of the town was traveling to legendary countries, the master was thundering forth two streets away because the house of prayer's door was closed. The storyteller smiled, and motioned to the servant, who remembered his mission and started running. At the sight of the latecomer, the rav exploded with anger and summoned him to explain himself.

"'There's a storyteller in the market and the whole town is listening to him, you should see how, ah it has to be seen ... Everyone who comes here to pray is sitting around and, if he finishes quickly, they should not be late.'

"'Open this door and bring me this peasant—I will have him flogged.'

"When the servant returned to the square, he was told that the storyteller had gone into the inn. The Baal Shem was waiting for him.

"He finished his drink and, holding his pipe, entered the abode of the Rav of Sharigrod.

"'Who do you think you are stopping people from going to prayers?'

"'Rabbi,' the Besht said calmly. 'There's no need to lose your temper. It would be better to sit down and make yourself comfortable, I'm going to tell you a story.'

'No, but...'

"The sentence remained on hold because the rabbi had just met the eyes of the Besht and he had not been able to resist such an expression.

"'During my travels, I always went with a team drawn by three horses: a bay, a piebald, and a white horse. None of these horses had ever neighed. One day, a farmer came to me and started shouting: Just slacken your reins! So that is what I did, Rabbi, I slackened the bridle and they started neighing. Have you understood that properly, Rabbi—the three horses, a bay, a piebald, and a white one, and not a single neigh, ever. And then there was this farmer, you catch the point, the good advice that he has given me, do you understand me?'

"'I understand,' the rav replied, trembling.

"And with that, he had not only understood but grasped that the storyteller was a *tzadik,* a diviner of the forgotten light. The rav sobbed, releasing a flood of hidden tears with his heart broken by the unfamiliar spring.

"'You will be carried higher!' said the Besht, before disappearing as if by magic."

And this story was the beginning of a real transformation. The rav gradually ceased his mortifications, continued to be rocked by the appearances of the Besht, and then, helped by his disciples, turned away from austerity for good, experienced joy, and atoned for the punishments he had inflicted. Having triumphed over his aggravations and sadness, he could help those who were cheerless.

Whosoever consents to be the diviner
of the lost light is righteous.
André Neher

The Heart's Delight Is a Woman!

I n the *mellah* of bygone Tetuan, two friends
had promised each other to marry their
children to one another later. One of the
friends became rich and had a daughter; the
other one raised his three sons the best he
could.

"Shall we do what we decided upon?"
the poor one asked one evening.

"And why not? But if you please, send
your sons to travel the world and let them
return with a good profession. Heftziba
will marry the most deserving brother."

Moreover, Ananias, the third son, and
the young girl loved one another. They
had exchanged vows in the presence of
the Lord. And this love in the eyes of life
was more natural and sound than an oath

taken by decree in the name of others, even if it were sealed by friendship.

Soon the three brothers took their leave, and the young girl lamented the departure of her lover and the uncertainty about the future. The brothers proceeded together for several days and arrived at Nador, where they rented a garret in a *fondouk*. They took each other by the shoulders, and wished each other a safe journey, and that they might find good masters and good professions. A pledge was made to meet each other again in this place and on this day in three years' time. One of the brothers boarded a boat at the port, while the second followed a caravan bound for Libya, and the third went along the coast toward the east.

Three years went by. On the appointed day, the three brothers kissed each other warmly. After a good supper, the eldest, Refael, described his journey.

"As I stand before you, I became a doctor. I learned from a wise man to treat the most hopeless cases, to listen to their souls in order to understand their ailments and treat them better, and to choose the plants the Lord has created to heal them. Here's the masterpiece comprising the formula mixed by my master that is known only to himself. This little flask can restore life. One day, I saw my master bring a dying man back to life in Cairo. I don't know who I shall save, blessed be this moment."

"How deserving you are," said his brothers.

"I went to Cordoba," Zera began, "the city where the great Averroes was born. I was of service to a famous astrologer there. He took me under his wing and opened the great book of the stars and magic to me. Look at this glass ball—I can see where I want and what I wish for in an instant."

"How deserving you are," said his brothers.

"As for me," said Ananias, "I met my master in the wool souks of Kairouan and I followed him into his workshop. He called me 'his son' and as he was old, he initiated me into an art that defies reason. Here's my leaving gift that he also wanted to be my wedding present." And the young man took out a square of wool that was admittedly woven skillfully, but it was drab.

"Don't frown my brothers, wait until you see, just take a look!"

Ananias climbed onto the carpet and flew away into the clouds. When he returned, a moment later, his brothers applauded.

"How deserving you are," they said, "a magic carpet ..."

"All I have to do is climb onto it and it takes me where I want, around the Mediterranean, to India, or the Antipodes."

They all three took each other by the shoulders.

The eldest said:

"We have no news of our parents. Zera, take out your glass ball."

"And see what Heftziba is doing," added the youngest.

The astrologer contemplated his ball and turned pale.

The faces of the parents were haggard and their eyes full of tears. In Heftziba's house, he saw her father kneeling, praying at his daughter's bedside, surrounded by melancholy figures.

Komo la roza en la guerta
I las flores sin avrir
Ansi ez una donzea
A las oras de murir.*

A dying girl
Is like a garden rose,
Among the unopened flowers.

"Is she . . . ?"

"No, I can see her chest rising, but how weak she is . . . "

"I could save her," said Refael. "I wish we were with her!"

"Entrust me with your flask," replied Ananias, leaping onto his magic carpet. "Thanks to us three, she will now be saved!"

"Go quickly my brother, here, take it!"

The lover poured the elixir over his beloved's lips straightaway. She opened her eyes and said:

"Oh my handsome friend, my tender fiancé, if you knew how life was slipping away by not seeing you anymore, *irme kero, irme kero a ti, adio* . . . I was dying from it. But you are here!"

Ananias' brothers arrived a few days afterward, and the worthy return of the three sons was celebrated. When the two friends discussed which of the brothers was

the most deserving, and they were about to select the eldest and his concoction, the two mothers conspired to intervene. They were there and had witnessed the miracle. Heftziba was dying from lovesickness, and it was the great happiness of seeing her lover again that had cured her. They winked at Refael and Zera, who understood them and then embraced their brother.

Life goes on, and the two fathers abided by their view because *the heart's delight is a woman!*

Ya boho kara de rosa, abyole la puerta.

And she with a rosy complexion, descends to open the door to him.
Traditional Judeo-Spanish song

* Traditional Ladino song

Where Have the Birds Learned Hebrew?

This is the story of a slightly mad Jew, Itzhak the street cleaner. He reigned over an old wheelbarrow and always applied himself diligently to his work, accompanied by an old dust-pan and a large scrubbing brush. Everyone knew him. He cut a cheerful disheveled figure, with an iron-grey beard, and two candid eyes like those of a dog. He really did have the look of a Jew. His haunted appearance added a commentary to the spectacle of his persona that was directed at the relentless slayers of the children of Abraham. It was almost as if life had replied with spirit: *You have mocked me, imitated and lampooned me, so here I am.* And the caricature that had become a man navigated the ludicrous side of life with honor, combining dignified sorrow and sacred joy in the splendor of his goodness. Rubbing his hands, he was looking out for the indefinable and for simplicity. This Jew was doubly sacred since he was a little mad and too Jewish to be true. He listened to the people in the street, and, while emptying his wheelbarrow of leaves, he jotted down the reflections in a notebook, the doubts, the jokes that are not always all that good, and extracted unanswered questions from them. He had clearly understood that all these Jewish celebrations, which governed the rhythm of the year, emerged like a hand from the clouds to nourish their hungry hearts. By means of an unusual alchemy, Itzhak had put his mind to founding his own religion and establishing his own festival, deriving the essence of holy days from his meditations as a disheveled road sweeper. He had witnessed the excitement preceding the birth of an infant, from the Passover; the white clothing and the eloquence of the *shofar*, from the festival of Rosh Hashanah; the ecstatic eruption of the carnival spirit, from the festival of Purim; the taste of fruits, from the Shavuot;

the tranquility of the leaves that fly and go where goodness sings to them, from the festival of Yom Kippur; pure joy without reason, from the festival of Sukkot; and the menorah, the ineffable light of the Tree of Life, from the festival of Hanukkah. And above all, he had incorporated into his own religion that was dedicated to the stars, the roar of laughter let out after the Sabbath; a benevolent hilarity that he wanted every day. When he went to the *choule,* the synagogue, far from seeking to imitate, understand, or participate, he took the unclassifiable emotions of his God from the peculiarities and the poetry of the Jews. Thus, Itzhak had declared a unique festival, written on an unlikely calendar, dictated by a star with an improvised tempo. All at once, there was a haphazard ceremony, when the Lord's arm rested on the shoulder of his madman, which was a sign that it was time to prepare the Tree of Life. Hence the unyielding man ceased toiling, and he prepared his velvet caftan, a scruffy old coat on which he fondly attached the pages he chose from his notebook. He had called this festival *the little paper slips.*

During those days, he strolled among the people, and the faithful laughed as they plucked off the sheets of paper from this strange brother whose pockets were full of beechnuts to distribute to the women and children. The taunts of those nearest to him stopped, and out of curiosity, perhaps out of respect, each person collected their message: *Where do words go after they have been said? Does the moon love me equally? How long does the rabbi's beard grow when he's asleep? Am I the good story? Who weeps for the rain? Can flowers sense us, if we ourselves are not breathing? Who turns my pages? What do we do with the whats? How many more? Where have the birds learned Hebrew?*

One day, when a righteous man was passing, he saw the festival of the madman and collected his message with the hand of friendship. The people watched from a distance, wondering which extravagant poem the wise man had taken and what would be the nature of the improbable exchange that was to ensue. They were astonished to see the wise man raise his eyes toward the sky, alternating kissing the madman's hand and having an obviously profound dialogue with loud bursts of laughter. Then the righteous man seemed to ask a question because he opened his hands in a gesture of anticipation. The road sweeper launched into a long monologue, rubbing his hands before opening them out as well. In turn, the righteous man embarked on an impassioned discourse. The ballet of hands and words continued for two and a half hours. It seemed as though two doctors of Law were engaged in a full juggling act with the Torah. Suddenly, the two men gripped each other by the arm and all at once started to dance. They whirled around so quickly that only one body of light could be distinguished.

> *Or ever I was aware, my soul made me*
> *like the chariots of Amminadib.*
> The Canticle of Canticles, VI, 12

> *Would I not be, for my good*
> *and for the good of everyone,*
> *the only one of my kind?*
> Itzhak, the road sweeper

The Night's Reply

T he Jewish tradition is acquainted with
great adventurers of the spirit, who are
able to live among the wild beasts, face the
solitude of the desert, or enter into the matrix
of a cave. Here they face the sky, all the forces
of the world, and themselves. Like the Yogis
of India or Tibet, like the *Kogi Mamos* of the
Sierra Nevada, the tzadikim penetrate the
illusion of light and search for the revelations
of the Torah or the secrets of the Kabbalah
in the darkness.

While Elijah lived in a cave and was fed
by ravens, Simeon Ben Yohai, pursued by
the Romans, fled with his son Eleazar to the
mountains to take refuge in a cave in Peki'in.
On the first night, with his head supported
by a rock and his body stretched out on the
ground, a thankful Simeon was watching
his son sleep. He was wondering how they
were going to survive. He fell asleep with
the thirst for knowledge and the desire to
nourish his soul. At dawn, he was woken

by the clear song of a spring and saw the branches of a carob tree bending under the weight of its pods. The night's reply carried the fruits from the sky and the earth. The belly of the cave hailed the indomitable pair to celebrate their spiritual rebirth.

Legend tells us that they removed their clothes, and buried themselves in the sand up to their necks in order to study the Torah. Their bodies adapted: they absorbed the inexpressible. For twelve years and twelve months, father and son dressed at prayer time and afterward laid their clothes on a rock. For twelve years and twelve months, they drank from the spring in this way, eating the fruits from the tree. Simeon had dispelled the mists that shrouded the secrets of evolution, had discovered the thirty-two paths of reintegration, and had understood what the exile of the Shekhinah meant and the mission of the tzadikim in this world. He had learned about fresh water, the seeds and the fruits of the carob tree, and to bless in the name of peace.

One night, Elijah arrived to announce to the two men that Hadrian the evil-doer was dead, and that the people were waiting for them to return to Tiberias. When Simeon and Eleazar came out of the cave, they were so radiant and their knowledge glowed to such an extent that they screwed up their eyes so as not to set the ground ablaze. As they proceeded along the paths of the Holy Land, their steps brightened up the ochre color, and the sand seemed to be made of gold.

In the East, anyone who utters Simeon Ben Yohai's name kisses his index finger, as a sign of reverence.

Wise Follies, Foolish Wisdom

E lijah was dancing in front of his stall. At night, all the shops run by Jews had been marked with a star, their windows whitewashed, and hateful statements put up on their walls.

"Have you gone mad, Elijah?"

"No, but I prefer to remain so."

The judge had just imposed a fine on Ana, as his attitude toward the sultan's procession as it went past was deemed misplaced.

"Instead of looking at me wide-eyed, do you understand the meaning of my judgment?"

" ...?"

"I am waiting!"

"What do you want me to reply? The sultan's judge inside my head still doesn't manage to be heard by the little Jew who jumbles up my language."

Moshe smiles on the threshold of his hut, in the *shtetl*, and holds the hand of a beautiful young girl, his very young wife.

"So," the angel said to him, "are you pleased?"

"Oh yes," replied Moshe, "very pleased!"

Then he thought otherwise:

"It's just with regard to my hut ..."

All at once, he wakes up with a start. He remembers that he's lying in his bed in his house at Krakow. He's a banker and his wife is sleeping next to him. He turns his head and he sees her triple chin wobble each time she exhales.

Then, he closes his eyes with all his strength and he calls the angel, desperately:

" ... my hut is perfect too!"

Three famous Jews are sitting in a train compartment. The first is a physicist named Albert Einstein and is playing with a small ball while watching the scenery flash by. The second is an eminent conductor of an orchestra. He sees the rivers, the trees, the fields, and the clouds pass by as if he was conducting a symphony. The third is the wandering Jew. He closes his eyes and remembers his next journey.

"Rebbe, Rebbe, do something, my son has gone mad!"

"Calm down, Esther, what has your son done this time?"

"He's now eating pork and he's frequenting a young girl who isn't Jewish!"

"Aha! He's not mad."

"Oh Rebbe, what would he do if he was mad?"

"He would frequent a pig and eat a young girl."

The Laughter of
the Light

Each man must go forth from Egypt,
every day.
The Maggid Rabbi Yisrael of Koznitz

S himon was a poor shoemaker. The law
forbad him to cultivate his patch of land
and the income from the old shoes he repaired
was barely enough to survive. His wife was
thin and his emaciated little children cried.
They were always hungry, trailing their colds
behind them like tree trunks. As the *babetskele*
who lived in the forest would say, "These
little ones blow their noses in the snow, and
their runny noses flow over Poland." Ah, if
he had possessed the means, he would have
bought a beautiful cow at the market, like his
neighbors, the *goyim* and the gardeners. The
land is generous, the cabbages and onions are
so easy to harvest for those who toil over it!

One evening, as he was getting ready to leave his hovel to entrust the ice-cold night and the darkness with his suffering, the door opened onto a handsome and noble old man. The old charmer placed a large bundle of zlotys on the table, stroked the hair of a sniveling little child, and withdrew without a word. Everybody was astounded and then the wife was enlightened and said:

"Shimon, it was *Eliahu Hanovi,* the prophet Elijah. She kissed her husband's forehead and took her children in her arms. Thus the wise man had come, Elijah with the thousand faces who knows what the future holds; the unforeseen with eyes filled with love. Shimon counted the bills and realized that they amounted to the cost of a fine heifer at the fair. And with that, he invented a *mayse,* a story, about a cow who flew through the air.

It's a blue heifer
Leave the door ajar!
Let those who are hungry come
And dance!

And his wife laughed, and he said to himself that it was good to see her teeth and that she was beautiful. The children started giggling, tearing away hardship. And here where the high priest is visible in the most sacred place *like a woman's breasts under a veil*, Shimon heard the loud laughter of God in the tabernacle of his hovel.

The slaves depart this year,
Next year, the free man.

The Wise Man's Nonsense

That night in the house of study, the atmosphere was inundated with questions and pointless rivalries. There were as many stars in the clear sky as there were feverish remarks. The young people spoke loudly—for two cents they would have liked to think of themselves as wise men. The old master knew that he had to imitate the bird-catcher from the story, in front of the open cage, and clap his hands so that the bird would find the way out. For whereas drowsiness is fatal to enquiry, verbosity and excitement impede the relaxation of the world. To shout, "Be silent," is a dangerous folly, as it appeals to childhood and the doors of laughter, seeking in a piece of nonsense what the law could not accomplish in such a case. He cleared his throat and the commotion ceased. In the place where Rabbi

Yehoudah had once roused his audience by means of an outrageous remark, the old master himself was going to circumvent their need for silence and emptiness with a torrent of nonsense. How refreshing.

"When I arrived in Poznán," he began, "I walked on the River Warta. As I had never seen a river, I thought it was a road."

The disciples were up to speed—their rabbi was going to provide them with one of his wonderful metaphors, unless he had genuinely walked on water . . .

"Then I bent down to pick up my prayer shawl and I fastened the water from the River Warta around my neck. As a fish was caught in my sleeve, I wanted to put it back on the road, but it said to me in Aramaic: 'Amen, Rabbi, put me down in Bialowieza Forest instead.' I took a step backward and I ended up being my own son; it was nighttime and the sun was shining on a wise old man who was sucking at his grandmother's breast, who was sitting on a rock, which was floating on some waves of leaves four meters in height."

The old rabbi eyed the ceiling but was imagining the dropped jaws of the young people and the knots they were tying themselves in as they listened. *Come on,* he thought, *let's see what there is in this torrent. Doesn't the wise man dive in with all his clothes on?*

"The old man of the forest said to me: 'Ah, here you are at last, I needed a shoemaker to renew the shoes of my oak trees. It's as well you're not married, as your wife could help my grandmother to sew the broken branches on again, and since you have no children, I should be blessed to welcome your eighteen daughters here.' I thanked him because a father is always concerned about his offspring and I put the boy I had found in the wife's mouth that I had not had, on the shoe of a tree busy splitting an axe in two. The wise man in front of me was so dazzling that I had to light a candle so that the sun would rise. I struck a match against the edge of a stream and divided myself into four to help it."

The master fell silent and glanced around to see what had become of his disciples. Apart from little Moshe, with a flicker of a smile crossing his lips, the others preferred to believe themselves to be mad than to dare to think that their rabbi had become so. *Come on, they are not ready yet, let's continue . . .*

"This is where things became complicated because I was four people! I shook my eight hands and wished myself good luck, but one of me maintained that they were not going to work on the Sabbath day. 'Who's saying anything about work?' replied the smallest me, who was mute. ME, the second me wrote in large letters on a leaf, because the smallest me was deaf. 'That's right,' shouted the third me, 'here they are like Hillel and Shamash who start again, oh fortunately I died yesterday!' The fourth me, who had yet to be born, moved his lips in his grave and prayed for the invisible words to find some fabrics with which to cover it. This is when I climbed up to the sky on a ladder of tears. It is from up there that I have seen you all, sitting on some flowers but sad like monkeys with pink bottoms."

Moshe was really laughing and several of them had eyes moist with tears, too. "I laugh, I cry." *Finally,* the master thought. And when he continued, they let themselves go, opening the doors of childhood and no longer holding back the benevolent hiccups.

"Just listen to the end of the story. All these events had given me an appetite; scarcely had I said a prayer when I saw a roasted goose fly under the cloud on which

I was sitting. I jumped on it and while it was bringing me back to Poznán, I ate three wings and six legs of my beautiful mount. We spoke in Yiddish and it told me I would soon be pregnant because I had swallowed a seed hidden in its side."

The rabbi was overtaken by a general sound of giggling.

"Wait," he said, before he too started bellyaching, while holding his stomach with both hands. "Wait," he repeated, and, taking hold of himself, said, "when I gave birth, my husband asked me where I had been during all this time."

"So what did you say?" Moshe burst out laughing amid the sound of chuckling.

"So, I said that I had been at the fair." "But it doesn't start until tomorrow," my husband said as he scratched his ear with one of his hind legs. "Perhaps" I replied, "but tomorrow we will celebrate the seventieth birthday of the dog and I would not want to miss that!"

Wiping away his tears of gold, the soul rejoiced; the wise old man glanced at the

Midrash Rabbah that was open at the Book of Genesis on his pulpit and smiled: it too said that "the heart carries the feet."

The Book
and the Face

The legend of Isaac Louria was intriguing. He was the great kabbalist thinker of Ashkenazic and Sephardic origins, who was born forty-two years after the exodus of the Jews from Spain to Jerusalem, and died in the prime of his life at Safed, in Galilee.

As a child, having followed his mother to Egypt, he quickly developed a passion for study in a *yeshiva* in Cairo and married at the age of fifteen. As he was very devout, he often went to the synagogue, where a seat was always reserved for him.

On that memorable day when the legend was born, a stranger occupied his chair. Isaac was upset, but he told himself that he had after all been given an opportunity here to sit right next to him, unassumingly, where there was a free seat. While he went into himself to observe the mysterious part that murmured to him *This is mine, this someone other than me is an intruder,* he was gripped by a burning curiosity, and leaned over to see the pages of the book the man held in his hands. And as soon as he caught a glimpse of the pages, everything around him disappeared—the synagogue and the faithful. He saw the mother letters dance with the double letters and the simple letters on the parchment, and he traveled on the carpet of the words of time. He heard singing, groaning that preceded and shouted joy. He saw the cosmos breathe; he saw the Lord retreat, casting his power of love and his exhalations into vases that break, with the divine sparks escaping from them and propagating as darkened prisoners inhabiting the whole of life. He saw the Shekhinah, the female face of God, glide from star to star across the lands of exile. Elsewhere, Isaac was juggling with the letters, playing with the words and the entire sentences, the remarks, as if they issued from a *rabab* or an *oud*. When he perceived the world once more, it was dark;

the prayer had finished hours ago and there was no stranger sitting in his chair. Only the book was open, with its numerous pages: the messenger had left it for him.

And there he was, secretly enlightened. He settled on a desert island on the Nile where his soul soared toward the atolls of infinity to meet his predecessors there.

Then he spoke of the mysteries that he has seen, and they were many that came to him. And as he had seen the letters dance, he read people's faces with an open book. He saw the unique and the unknown, the beauty of this other that is prayer.

True Beauty

I t happened, because I have seen it. And
when I described it to the people I met
along the way, they listened to me near the
fire, and said: "*Alevie,* that should happen to
us, both to me, and to you."

I always start my vigils by telling the
story of the "three wishes," the one about
the legendary night, on the seventh day
of Sukkot, the *Hoshana Rabbah,* where
three little Jewish children squander their
wishes at the precise moment when the
door to Heaven opens. Later, at dusk,
they sing *Iaïbaïbaï Baïiabababababaï* and the
dairyman Aaron cries out: "*Alevie,* that
should happen to us, both to me, and to
you!"

Then, I go through this story about
Golem, who protects the children of the
most High from the Cossack hordes and
tells of a *Bobe Ha,* that swivels around on
her chicken legs, to make them shudder.

Then I cite Rabbi Hune of Kolochitz: "Nothing and nobody down here frightens me; not even an angel, not even the angel of fear. But the moaning of a beggar makes me shudder."

Thus, everyone is ready to hear this mysterious story extracted from the dreams of Rabbi Nahman, a parable drawn from his own life of joy and suffering that I open with this quotation by Mendel of Kotzk: "God dwells wherever we let God

in." And each time I tell it, a spark, a flash comes to me: I glimpse for a moment the mystery of hidden things through the veil. I entrust it to the Book, because I hope to take you to this place where observations whisper, with their meaning renewed at each reading, in order to keep women and men anchored to the wind. *Mazel Tov!*

God dwells wherever we let God in.

A king liked to wonder secretly whether there was a man like him, anywhere in the world, who was escaping the thousand torments of existence. He himself had the best of this world as it was he who possessed the power. Was there a being capable of dominating the bitter grasses, and the quicksand that naturally beset humankind? One evening, he went out in the middle of the night to unearth the rare pearl. Hidden from view, he searched every house, and absorbed the words that make the universe shudder, investigated the flesh of the lamenting voices, inhaled the beings in the morass together with their cries. The groan of a merchant fearing that he would see his business founder rose from an opulent-looking home. From a dwelling further on rose the prayer of a woman for her desperate, unemployed husband; further on, the tremulous voice of a rich man in debt to the royal crown could be heard.

The night was inundated with groans, sobs, sighs, and unsteadiness in the face of the tenacious army of minor and major torments. As he continued on his way, he saw a low-lying house, a kind of hut set into the earth. Part of the roof was missing and the shelter featured some windows opening toward the ground. The king noticed a man sitting inside. He was holding a violin in his hands and he was playing it in a strange way, emitting a reedy sound that was almost inaudible. The king was in no doubt that the singular musician was brimming over with joy, as the wine in the clay vase was in pride of place on the table amid the exquisite dishes that were daintily arranged. This man was exultant—nothing was coming to torment him.

The king crept into the shelter and called out to the violinist, as he wanted to make sure that there was no bitterness present, not even a tiny amount, and no muddy footprint was coming to spoil the delightful feast. The words spoken by the musician were magnificent and terribly clear, and he took two goblets from the pleasing tableful of food, offering one to the king, who proposed a toast, and he too drank in the name of friendship.

Assured of finally keeping this man cheerful, the king lay down on a bed and, free from any agitation, all at once fell into a deep sleep. In the early hours of the morning, he woke up with a start, in a rush to leave this wonderful shelter, and asked the violinist where he had acquired the unbroken dishes he had used for his delightful feast.

"I know how to replace fragments, and restore each object that has been damaged," replied the musician. "I don't have the power to create something from nothing, but I was born to repair anything that has been shattered. Every day, I go in search of objects that men have broken during the night, and I collect the five or six matching pieces to make these repairs; I buy this fountain of wine, and these succulent fruits that you have seen me drink and eat."

When he heard these words, the king's heart was agitated, and he muttered his intention to poison the musician's happiness, returning to his palace straightaway.

At that very moment, he summoned his scribes and laid down the terms of a decree, in one fell swoop, that was addressed to all his subjects without exception. So that nobody could be unaware of the law, a notice was displayed with the words: *It is strictly forbidden for the owners of broken objects to have them repaired by anyone at all.* Everybody would have to cobble them together and patch them up themselves or obtain new ones.

When the violinist began his rounds, he was accosted by his regular customers who informed him of the new decree. He was accustomed to making every effort to undertake all the restoring and mending within the kingdom, in addition to the tiniest of objects. The musician was afflicted by the order and found it unjust and excessive, but he had faith in the most High. Along the way, he saw an eminent, middle-class citizen decked out like a lumberjack. He hadn't found anyone to hire who would fell his trees and was getting ready to do it himself.

"This is not a task for you," the musician said to the rich man. "I'm going to help you cut this wood." After he had done this and had earned one coin, he was delighted with his new trade; he found other forest owners, and in a few hours he had raised the six coins he needed to put on the delightful feast. He trembled and his face lit up in front of the fountain and the flavorful fruits that were displayed in his shelter.

The night was jet-black when the king appeared at the window. The musician was brimming over with joy, and rejoiced—nothing was coming to torment him. The sovereign entered stealthily, then lay down on a bed and fell asleep. In the morning, disillusioned, he whispered:

"How did you organize your delightful feast, what fresh produce did you acquire?"

"I had gone to repair objects that have been shattered. I went to the place where cracked objects and shattered fragments pile up; I learned from the public about the king's decree forbidding them to call upon my services."

"And weren't you gripped by anger?"

"I relied on the Lord and I occupied myself with cutting wood all day."

"And afterward?"

"This is enough to buy what I need."

With these words, the king was in a very bad mood and proclaimed another decree, addressed to all his subjects, this time forbidding them to have recourse to lumberjacks.

When the violinist began his rounds, he agreed to this new decree and was employed to do housework, earned his pittance, and was cheerful once more. The following morning, the dismayed king issued a new decree, and patiently the musician continued on his way, and found a position as a servant in exchange for his six coins and was in good spirits once more. Certain that he would unravel the thread leading to the musician's defeat, the king forbade any recourse to servants. Thus, the friend of harmony became a soldier, and was enlisted during the day and dressed in the uniform of the royal guard.

Every day he was entrusted with a mission and a sword. But when the king understood how the man was carrying on his resplendent life, he had the army's coffers closed before any pay could be given to the soldiers. Bumping into the kindly treasurer, in the face of his calm tenacity, he was promised double pay for the following day, as the royal decree only applied to this day alone.

The musician went away keeping his uniform. A little later, deftly removing the pommel from his sword, he made a similar piece of wood to match, and fit the perfect replica onto the blade. He went to see the pawnbroker, and offered him the genuine ceremonial pommel. The old man examined the delicately carved work, and he counted out the coins one by one as the violinist perused the unchanging furrows of time across his brow. At nightfall, despite his misfortune, he was laughing, and like a light in the darkness he reached his shelter with something to feast on, and he trembled at the sight.

The king arrived, and deeming the leftovers of the feast to be a distressing scene, he remained prostrate. In the morning, he listened to the violinist and was overwhelmed by his music.

In the palace, he summoned the minister for justice and his tribunal in order to conduct an execution that very day, which they would have to improvise in the prison courtyard. He named the violinist as the executioner and put him in charge of carrying out this irrevocable sentence: only he would cut off the condemned man's head. The minister summoned the violinist while the king mustered his government to make the matter public and humiliate the man, who knew how to tremble, in front of the entire kingdom. When the violinist found himself in the presence of all the assembled dignitaries, he questioned them about the nature of his summons.

"This evening," the king replied, "you will behead a man."

"My life is dedicated to life, I have never shed anyone's blood. Find someone other than me who could be an executioner."

"Upon my word," said the king, savoring the moment, "there's a first time for everything, and here you are, hired to kill."

Naively, the musician continued:

"The sentence seems to have been passed by the tribunal. Was it fair? How can you be really sure? I am obliged to do something that I have never contemplated nor carried out. How can I deprive a fellow creature of their life if they are innocent?"

"Everything is perfectly in order," said the king. "It's also true that you will be the executioner. This man shall die."

Seeing that he had no power over the will of the king, the violinist prayed fervently and left it up to the only true judge who knows the hearts of men.

"Oh Lord, you whose eyes are constantly turned toward the Truth, you who creates all the musical instruments of the world, I have never shed any blood. If the man I have been ordered to kill is indeed innocent, change my weapon into a branch."

Then all at once, the violinist pulled the sword from its scabbard and the entire room was shaken with resounding and life-saving laughter.

The musician had merely unsheathed a minstrel's bow, made from the kind of wood with a touch that makes the soul tremble.

Only then did the king see the true beauty of the violinist and let him go in peace.

The Lord's House

Nouriel was sitting on a bench in joyous communion with the stars. The urchin loitered with the wandering Jews and the Tziganes. But in the evening, he liked being alone with the sky. As he was bright, the rabbi from the shtetl enjoyed teasing him.

"So Nouriel, does the sky's kippa suit you better than that of the tailor? Tell me, as you frequent the musicians of our entire galaxy—show me where the house of the Lord is located."

"*Azoy?*"

"Yes, really. It interests me. For all that I am a rabbi! I'd like to know where the songs of the wretched go that you frequent!"

"Rebbe, can you show me a single blade of grass or a single star where the Lord does not reside?"

"No, I cannot, Nouriel. This is why we dance with the *klezmer*. Our earthly bodies soar into a state of joy and into a circle of dance toward the heavenly bodies. In the garden of souls, not one thing can be isolated and even suffering starts to dance. The sparks ascend and light up to encourage us.

The Patience and Impatience of Wise Men

We know this story about the proverbial patience of Hillel, when two men had bet on the wise man's wisdom. Urged to answer ludicrous questions asked by the rascal who wanted to annoy him in the midst of his preparations for the Sabbath, the wise man had remained unruffled, open and friendly.

It's not a wager that caused Samuel Sousrati to demonstrate one day that patience could be pushed beyond reasonable limits, and yet turn out to be beneficial. The wise man had found the jewels the queen of Italy had lost; the sovereign had promised to provide a substantial reward to the person who returned this treasure within a period of thirty days, however. The person who brought it back any later would be executed. And yet Rabbi Samuel waited until the deadline had expired. He arrived at the palace with the jewel box, taking responsibility for his lateness, the consequences of which he knew, and didn't offer any excuse or beg for mercy.

"Were you absent from Rome, did you think that you would be accused of fleeing?" said the queen.

"No," replied the wise man. "I did not want Her Majesty to think that I had hurried because of fear. It is clarity that guides a man to do what he must do, and not spinelessness and blackmail. I only tremble in the presence of the Lord."

"It is I who am rewarded for knowing you—you and your God," replied the queen, as she handed him a purse, thereby revoking even her own decree.

Sometimes patience is imposed by the wise man, even without his knowledge, on the man who is quick to lose his temper.

A Jew was praying by the side of the road when the governor went by and greeted the man, without receiving any answer. Irritated, he repeated his greeting and, seething with anger, he waited until the Jew had at last finished muttering.

"I could have you skinned for your insolence."

"Without wishing to offend you, if you were with the king and a friend had hailed you, would you have answered him?"

"No."

"And if you had behaved like this, perhaps you would have been suspended from a horse's tail and dragged through the dust."

"It's possible."

"I was in communion with the King of kings; please forgive me as you would have liked your friend to have forgiven you. I wish you good day as well."

His reply pleased the governor, who went away smiling.

The patience and impatience of wise men can even lead to the extraordinary.

Some Hasidim were walking along the road, describing the miracles they had witnessed. One of them related how his rebbe had dissuaded them from making a run for it when a big storm was brewing. "Wait patiently," he had said, "I concern myself with the impatience of the rain. If the downpour is eager by nature, we should be wary of making any great haste!" He made an illustrious gesture, and using his cane he marked out a dry strip between the shoulders of the road. The rain was falling on either side of them, while they themselves were walking in the dry.

Another disciple recalled one evening how just before the Sabbath he was in a carriage with his master and they were going to be caught out after dark. Should they stay for hours sitting in the heart of the forest, as traveling during the feast of the Sabbath was impossible? His master took his cane and gestured, separating patience and impatience. Night fell on either side of the path, where it was the Sabbath. The unshakeable and generous sun kept shining on the road like a beacon. For several miles, the village women prepared to bless the candles, but the colors of the day were restored. The clocks counted down the timeless retinue, and the ravens watched the higher forces disrupt the natural laws.

"When we arrived," the young disciple added, "the people understood why the sun had made the Sabbath wait."

The Three Questions

From the Babylonian Esther Midrash

A king, who was determined to build a city, presented the place he had chosen for this impressive project to his astrologers and his magicians. The magicians approved this choice, but they set down a condition, so that the town would be well-built and prosperous. A child was to be walled up alive in the foundations and offered for this purpose by its mother, of her own free will. Three years passed, and one day an old woman came forward with a child, in order to offer him. He was about ten years old, with bright eyes and a high forehead. Before he was walled up, he addressed the king in a clear voice:

"Allow me to ask three questions of your wise men. If their answer is truthful, it's because they will have read the signs well. Otherwise, they will have lost their way."

The king consented:

"Astrologers," continued the child, "what are the lightest, the sweetest, and the hardest in the world?"

The magicians withdrew for three days and gave their response.

"The lightest is a feather, the sweetest is honey, and the hardest in the world is a stone."

The boy burst out laughing, with his face turned toward the sun.

"Anyone here could have answered that without any reflection. Be warned that the lightest thing is a child in the arms of its mother, as it cannot be heavy. Isn't the sweetest thing the milk this mother has for this child? The hardest thing you could ever imagine in this world is that one day she has to offer the child to be buried alive."

The astrologers were astounded; the boy's answer was truthful.

They marveled at how they had lost their way and how they had neither understood the signs nor listened to the stars. The child was spared and the generation that listened to the child was rewarded.

The Legend Springs from a Woman

O ld Mordechai shook his head. The maxim that promised misfortune to the father who only has daughters was debatable, even with reference to the handing down of wisdom. The idea that a son was preferable to Adifa seemed foolish to him. He was gratified and proud to be the father of the great-great-granddaughter of Havah, the mother of all life. It is with joy and attentiveness that he had taught her the Torah, this gem given to the children of Israel. He had known how to let her savor these passages in which Sarah rouses Abraham so that he dismisses Ishmael; where Rebekah understands the destiny of her sons and takes action so that Jacob receives the blessing of Isaac. He had passed on to her the fervor and strength of Leah, the boldness of Rachel, and the courage of Tamar. These women turned the established order upside down. As Adifa had not had her mother at her side, he spoke to her about Jochebed and Miriam, the mother and sister of Moses, respectively—midwives who took care of the baby boys the Pharaoh wanted to see perish. Many a time, he had read the Scroll of Esther to his daughter and expressed his admiration for the woman who had saved her people by marrying the king of Persia, and had turned the festival of Purim into their favorite celebration.

Old Mordechai was proud of seeing his daughter stand up to the scholars, arguing about claiming a matrimonial right favorable to wives; a right that fully notices the woman who blossoms out into herself. Adifa had been raised in wisdom, taught about the danger of a rigid judgment without sensitivity or understanding. Thus the young girl was ready to be this *ezer kenegdo* who creates a breach in the potential of existence, like a strange tale of ancient times. Whereas

the law urged a man to get married, have children, and make some decree or other, it asked a woman to be the storyteller of the *Thousand and One Nights* of otherness. As the old man liked to say when he thought about Chimra, his late wife—*the legend springs from a woman*; the legend of a man able to understand, and of a woman, who, informed of her role, can be induced to rouse him with love.

Tsouriel was a bright young man. Adifa and Tsouriel had lived in the same street and shared the same games. For a long time, they knew that they were pledged to each other, by their silences and their words. Tsouriel was rather athletic and enjoyed running across the crests of the hills and meditating facing the sun. He had a flowing mane of hair and seemed like a creature of the sands. The company of gazelles and an inner fire met his needs. Without Adifa's penetrating gaze and her determination to see him grow in wisdom, he would certainly not have studied very much. She wasn't impervious to his vigor, but partial to a battle of wits.

She knew the possibilities smoldering in him; she carried and nurtured the seeds of potential in her breast, and would even protect these seeds from him. She wanted him to exist beyond his limits and not be a desperately solitary wise man.

Therefore, at first he had studied for the sake of the gentle eyes of Adifa, and then he had developed a liking for it alongside the discipline.

This strength of the young animal combined with knowledge turned the young man into a most esteemed scholar. The sultan chose him to be one of his advisers and, after one year, he married Adifa under the watchful eye of old Mordechai. However, as Tsouriel had gained self-assurance and was wary of his wife's candor, he insisted that she did not meddle in his affairs. Their love was noble, and their embraces were pure and strong, but a kind of inflexibility was beginning to take hold of the young wise man's heart. He drew up a contract stipulating that any intrusion by his wife into his affairs would put an end to their marriage. She had dreaded this moment, but complied on one condition: If she broke the oath, she would take away what she judged to be the most precious.

"As the Torah is my witness," she said, "a man is equal to a woman. Didn't wives refuse to sell their jewelry to the Golden Calf and then donate it all to build the Temple? If I am rejected, then I will take away what is most dear to me."

Tsouriel smiled, because as far as he was concerned nothing like that could happen. He loved her so much and he just wanted to avoid a cleft in his rock opening up.* He consented.

And the inevitable happened. Six months later, a man was arrested and accused of plotting against the sultan. Tsouriel was put in charge of conducting the investigation. Although the evidence was unreliable, he was inclined to favor a conviction, but was still hesitating.

"Have you questioned the lying witnesses?" Adifa said, as they were having a meal.

"Don't concern yourself with that, all right?"

"Do you remember what you said: 'It is better to be among the persecuted than in the house of the persecutors.' In this case, some powerful people are lying."

"Will you keep silent?"

"Death and life are in the power of the tongue!"

"You have broken our agreement!"

"You would do better to run off into the hills and afterward deliver your justice."

He ran off into the hills and heeded his conscience. He reported to the sultan that false evidence was making him inclined to favor a verdict of not guilty. But there was a cleft in the rock and his heart was too wounded for him to choose the flexible path. With his eyes full of tears, he signed the deed of repudiation.

"Give me one more evening and night. I'll leave tomorrow," she said.

At mealtime, she poured a few drops of a sleeping draught into his glass. They went to bed. He had only just embraced her, with tears in his eyes and biting his lips so that he would not shout out his love to her, when he started snoring.

She had prepared everything very skillfully. Old Mordechai arrived with a servant and they carried the sleeping man off into a cave they had made ready.

When Tsouriel awoke, angry and chained to the wall, he started shouting and sent his flask, bread, and prayer shawl flying.

It wasn't until the third day that she came, and brought some provisions and some fresh water. She handed him his shawl.

"What have you done?" he said. "You have abducted the sultan's adviser!"

"No. I have merely taken away what I want and is most dear to me."

" ...?"

"My noble husband—an agreement is an agreement."

She came to see him every day. He prayed hard, until he perceived the spring that was flowing in the hollow of his name.

He heard the laughter of understanding.
The chain was transformed into water and
the legend springs from a woman.

* *Tsouriel* means the rock of God, imperfection,
spring.

The True Gift

Hillel the Babylonian, the esteemed wise man, one day set out a problem for his students that would require them to interweave their knowledge of the mind and the way of the heart with one and the same answer:

"A man has just earned a thousand dinars, and he deducts three hundred from this amount in order to give it to the poor. How much does he have left?"

"Seven hundred," replied the students, confident of their response.

"No, you don't know how to count. This is not how a man's fortune is assessed. The seven hundred dinars will be swallowed up by levies, heirs, taxes, and thieves, and not to mention a potential fire or an earthquake. Nobody can claim that the money passing through their coffer or their pocket is a possession acquired on a long-term basis. *Here today, gone tomorrow.*

The actual amount of credit that the man earns is three hundred dinars. Thus says the Lord when he assesses a man's fortune: he records his gifts.

"My mission on earth is to discover what I lack inside myself, outside of myself, and finally to fill it." said Rabbi Menachem Mendel: the response to the problem set out by Hillel the Babylonian is still relevant.

Wall-Wall

For my father

René Kaleb Goldman was looking at the Wailing Wall, where he had just been praying in his own way. Because for this improbable Jew, who was a socialist, a non-Zionist who had emigrated to Israel, a layman who liked the Torah, full of humor, a commentator on Groucho Marx and Albert Einstein, an accordionist, and the spitting image of Woody Allen, this wall was the very place where he could entrust his being and his oddness to God. As for God, he understood.

He had come to plead with God on behalf of his Arab neighbors, for little Aouicha and her old grandfather, in order that the steel horses should spare their tiny house. René had put his kippa aside, just like the Parisian cap he had worn for

forty years. He had rested his forehead against the place where the stone cries as a result of being pounded by souls. He had stroked the edges with his fingertips, patted the little hollow where he was going to deposit his letter to the Merciful One who sees everything, and who knows that a human being that observes his laws attains eternal life through the gradient of kindness, whether Jewish or not. God, who had created two loins like two pitchers for Abraham, two springs so that he learns the Torah alone in the night—had he not conceived humankind to love in peace? René Kaleb let his heart open up like a fresh walnut, and he shed the water of his tears, suffused with the lingering wail of the exiled people. "May they wear sidelocks, chapkas, or live here, be Arabs and too near the other wall, the old grandfather and little Aouicha. Lord, I am what I am. ... You have made me Jewish, a socialist of the whole world. Help me to gather enough daughters and sons of Israel to protect the tiny house. I beseech you to create a story out of this day. How can the Temple be rebuilt on the ruins of inhumanity? How much do we have left?"

All the important things that I have been able to obtain cannot, in my eyes, compete, in the face of one minute of love.
Rabbi Nahman of Bratslav

Chemeche's
Trap Door

Make the violins of the *shetl* weep, make the clarinettes of the *klezmer* laugh, I want to tell you the tale of the old storyteller Chemeche, the immortal *mentsh,* who collects restorative stories and causes the silence to dance between the words.

At the back of his hut, the prattler enters a small alcove, which is however larger than the world. Here, he placates his sense of reason and flies into this unreasonable universe where love is stronger than death. Secretly, he rectifies this part of the world, which he has custody of, and where he tends to the past. How did he dare release this door trusted by madmen, this trap door lodged in the head where the light streams forth, which sees everything, from the beginning to the end of time; a small groove left under the lips where the angel

places a silent finger by decree and where enraged people place their boot?

Here's the reason. He was there, in the Warsaw ghetto, on the day when four thousand children were taken from the orphanages to board the death trains. He saw Janusz Korczak, the old doctor, author, and educator, walking calmly with his one hundred urchins toward the cattle trucks. In this silent, dignified protest, in this procession of small children who were wiser than the wise men, stronger than the powerful, a choir could be heard singing *The Lady of Warsaw*, the melody of the desolate. The entire ghetto held its breath. The most destitute recovered their share of dignity for a moment. Then the fiends yelled and did the only thing they knew how, and handled the children roughly. As they were crying, the old doctor said to them: "It will pass, everything passes, don't be afraid." Then they remembered the tales about King Matthias, and King Solomon's engraved ring. The sadistic officer could do nothing about it: when wisdom and kindness walk through darkness and *once upon a time* precedes them, love is stronger.

Chemeche, who witnessed the tragedy, wavered between madness and death, when the trap door in his head opened up. The angel took away his finger before the enraged man could place his boot. And Chemeche became a *seer*, both invisible and immortal. He staggered along as he left the ghetto and wandered as far as his hut deep in the woods. He wept for a long time and so profusely that large bears came in to give him comfort, and the beech and oak trees caressed him with their branches, and the birds with their wings and their songs. His heart opened up and the spring of his word started flowing. In springtime, he built the alcove in the back of the hut, and from then on and throughout time, he raises the familiar trap door and brings back stories full of hope.

To What Do I
Owe the Honor?

*May your prayer be a window
that opens onto the sky.*
Levi Yitzchak of Berditchev

*The answer is yes.
But what was the question?*
Woody Allen

He came from nowhere and he was going God knows where, peddling rebellious ideas as much as healing herbs or amulets; he was a wandering, wise hobo, with a beggar's bag on his shoulder, gathering sparks. He was a creature of habit—in Prague, Katowice, Lutsck—he knew where to sleep and eat. And when he was traveling from Olsztyn to Vilnius, he stopped for a few days on the shore of a lake to give thanks. He was a strange man and his prayer was equally so. It was uttered during Yom Kippur. Moreover, a rabbi from Masuria had consulted a soothsayer to find out what prayer had ascended to the highest during the festival, and which Jew had been heard in the fields of the sky. The soothsayer had prophesied that the man would be found in a hut, on the shore of a lake at a certain location. The rabbi set off and soon found himself in front of the extraordinary little hut where the son of Bohemia had his refuge. Imagine his surprise to discover a tall, bearded, half-naked man warming himself by the fire.

"Come in, rabbi, but be careful not to heat the landscape. Shut this door for me!"

At the astounded gaze of his visitor, the tall curmudgeon said that he had just had a ritual bath.

"I cannot bear bathing huts and bath houses. I like to take my *mikva* in the company of the sky and the fish," he said, as he took the liberty of shoving his visitor robustly in the back. "To what do I owe the honor, rabbi? Oh, so it's true, eh—have you lost your synagogue so that you can come and nose around here like this, or did you leave on the quiet with the candelabrums? No, I'm having a bit of fun. I am a peculiar *mentsh* . . . But I am me, ah yes, in the presence of the Lord and no other."

"I . . ."

"You're right, we should first propose a toast; the news is good! The peasants are beginning to shake this earth like an old carpet."

"Um . . ."

"You're not wrong there."

The rabbi was sweating profusely in front of the hearth. For, ultimately, had he come over to ask a question or not? Or . . . was it his visit that was the question? Or the question he had not yet asked that he had just had answered? This tall, thin man seemed to be drawn from a story about these wandering devotees about whom he didn't know what to think. After clearing his throat, he ventured to speak to him.

"My friend, did you pray intensely during Yom Kippur?"

"Tell me something, rabbi, do I ask you whether the rebbetzin prepares some *blintzes* or *gefilte fish* for the Sabbath? Am I not allowed a little privacy? You come into my home, and I have no time to put my pants on. Do you want to see my tongue or under my arms? You are one strange *kibitzer!*"

"Er, I didn't mean to be inquisitive ..."

"When I speak with God, that is my concern; it's private."

"It's just that after I had consulted a soothsayer, it was revealed to me that your prayer ascended so high that ..."

"That you fell out of the sky onto your buttocks, *Hou ha!*"

"That's it," replied the rabbi, encouraged by the tall bearded man to laugh.

"*Oy-oy-oy!* And you'd like to know what I have said and done?"

"If ..."

"If I wish it, good; here we are in agreement."

First, I pray quickly. I look upward with my back straight and I say, *Adonai,*

I have made you a large parcel containing all the times that I have spoken to you about along the paths this year. I have deposited my silences, my laughter, and my sorrows all together, wrapped up in the fresh air. I have added some faces. I would like you to alleviate their sorrows. Ay-ay-Ay, do this for your louftmentsh. Thank you for each day when I wake up in this country so far from you, and yet so beautiful, that you have given to me. That's it. After that, I throw the parcel as high as I can in spirit, above what is visible and even what is imaginable, to the country without a country."

"I'm very glad to have left my synagogue for a while," the rabbi replied. "May I go and bathe in your, er ... in your *mikva?*"

Thy way is in the sea, and thy path in the great waters, and thy footsteps are not known.
David, Psalm 77, 19

The Wisdom of
the Dawn

The old master had assembled his students and other young people from the village to say goodbye to them and to leave them with a pearl of wisdom during an absence that could be long. To travel so far and at that age was not without risk; therefore, this departure for the Holy Land had the feel of a farewell as their faces were solemn and their hearts silent.

"Well then, don't pull a long face. If you want to please me, you should dance later! I have one thing I would wish to entrust you with, so that you take care of it." The sound of whispering could be heard spreading through the gathering. Each person was ready to watch over the master's treasure.

When he took out his handkerchief, they were expecting to see a small box, a book, or a precious object appear.

"It's not a material thing that I want to entrust you with. It's a question, a simple question for you to preserve, nurture, and cherish. My children, when can you be really certain that the night is over and the dawn is breaking?"

"When the first ray of sunlight appears?"

"No."

"When the cock crows!"

"Neither."

"When you can distinguish a ewe from a dog?"

"No."

" . . . an olive tree from a jujube tree?"

"Hey no!"

"You can be certain that the night is really over and the dawn is breaking when you see a stranger coming and when you know, without doubt, that he is our brother. At that moment we are enlightened. Who is wise—is it the educated man? The man or woman who learns from any man, is wise.

Glossary

Abbasids: dynasty of Sunni caliphs.

Abergel: in Arabic, "a one-footed man"; *vergel* is an orchard in Spanish.

Adonai: The Eternal, the Lord.

Aggadah, pl. Aggadot: parable, legend, wisdom that captures the attention of the audience.

Al-Andalous: Iberian peninsula under Muslim rule.

Aljamía: mixture of Arabic script and Romance language; dialect.

Ashkenazi: Jew originating from central Europe and the East.

Ay-ay-Ay: Yiddish: In this context, expresses enthusiasm.

Baal Shem Tov: founder of Hasidism, Jewish mystical movement.

babetskele: a little old woman, a grandmother.

Besht: abbreviation for Baal Shem Tov.

blintzes: Yiddish: filled pancakes.

Bobe Ha: ambivalent creature; witch that can devour or aid the hero of a tale.

Canticles of Canticles: poem; King
    Solomon's love song.

cholent: meat dish with vegetables,
    simmered for a very long time.

Djoha: foolish, wise man and antihero
    known by the Judeo-Spanish.

Djohaya: Djoha's sister, rebellious friend of
    the people.

double letters: expressing duality; seven
    letters in total.

ezer kenegdo: a helper for him, a helper
    against him.

fondouk: caravanserai, a stopping-place for
    caravans.

gefilte fish: stuffed carp.

Golem: mythical creature created by the
    hand of man, animated by the magical
    use of a divine name.

goyim: non-Jews.

hammam: steam bath establishment.

Hanipol (of): Polish lineage and region of a
    Hasidic movement.

Hanukkah: Jewish festival of lights.

Hasid, –im: follower of the joyous
    communion with God (Eastern
    Europe).

Havah: Eve.

hidden tzadikim: thirty-six Righteous
people (*Lamed Vav*), who appear in each
generation and maintain the world in
life.

hou ha: Yiddish: ironic in this context.

Kabbalah: reception of the Law; mystical,
secret knowledge of Judaism.

kibitzer: in this context, an inquisitive
person who meddles in the affairs of
others.

kippa: small skullcap used by Jews to cover
their heads.

klezmer: Traditional music of the
Ashkenazi Jews.

klops: meat loaf.

kuchen: a cake.

Lady of Warsaw (the): old Polish song that
became revolutionary.

louftmentsh: Yiddish: dreamer, poet.

maassiot: *the stories,* Hebrew word with a
dual meaning; deeds and tales.

maggid: storyteller, who derives meaning
and virtue from his tales.

Marrane: name given by the Spanish to
the Jews and Arabs converted by force.

mellah: Jewish quarter.

menorah: candelabrum.

mentsh: a man, and by extension of
meaning, an admirable individual.

midrash: collection of commentaries, tales,
and parables surrounding the biblical
text.

mikva: ritual bath.

Modé ani léfanékha: Hebrew: the
beginning of the morning prayer, lit. *I
offer thanks before you.*

mother letters: Aleph, Mem, Shin:
Hebrew mother letters of revelation.

Mozarab: Christian minority of the Al-
Andalous.

Olam Habba: the world to come.

oud: lute.

oy-oy-oy: Yiddish: and how!

Passover: Pesach, festival celebrating the
exodus from Egypt.

Purim: festival of lots, the deliverance of the
Jewish people from Persia.

Ra'hamana: *He who answers those with a
broken heart*; the Merciful.

rabab: vielle and lute.

Rabbi Nahman of Bratslav: eminent *tzadik* who taught through stories.

rabbi: my master.

rav: leader of the religious community.

rebbe: master, Hasidic teacher.

rebbetzin: rabbi's wife.

remedy tales: tales of awakening, veils of the Torah for Rabbi Nahman.

Rosh Hashanah: Jewish New Year, first day of Tishri, anniversary of the world's creation.

Sabbath: day of rest and prayer, from Friday evening to Saturday evening.

Sephardi: Jew originating from the Iberian peninsula, North Africa, the Balkans, Greece, Turkey, Israel.

Shavuot: the pilgrimage festival marking the giving of the Torah on Mount Sinai.

Shekhinah (the): the female face of God; the divine presence.

Shelomo: Solomon.

Shir Hashirim: the *Song of Songs*.

shofar: instrument, ram's horn.

shtetl: Yiddish: a small town, a large village, a convivial area for Jews.

simple letters: expressing the organs and
  directions; twelve letters in total.
Song of Songs: another name for the
  Canticle of Canticles.
Sukkot: Feast of Booths or harvest festival.
synagogue: Place of worship, study, prayer,
  community life.
Torah: divine teaching received by Moses,
  both written and oral; living law
  handed down and developed across the
  generations.
Turkish delight: eastern confection.
tzadik: a Righteous one.
Wandering Jew (the): legendary figure.
yeshiva: study center of sacred texts.
Yom Kippur: or Day of forgiveness, Day of
  Atonement, festival of forbearance.
Zatsal: abbrev. "May the memory of the
  righteous be a blessing."

Sources

Bloch, Muriel, *Contes Juifs*, Circonflexe, Paris, 2009.

Bouganim, Ami, *Le Rire de Dieu*, Points Seuil, Paris, 2010.

Buber, Martin, *Les Récits hassidiques*, Points Seuil, Paris, 1996.

Buhler, Alain, *L'Adieu aux enfants*, Olivier Orban, Paris, 1978.

Carrière, Jean-Claude, *Le Cercle des menteurs*, Plon, Paris, 1998.

Citati, Pietro, *La Lumière de la nuit*, l'Arpenteur, Mayenne, 1998.

Estin, Colette, *Contes et fêtes juives*, Beauchesne, Paris, 1987.

Fischmann, Patrick, *Contes et légendes de la musique, du chant et de la danse*, Royer, Paris, 1998: *Contes des sages nomads*, Points Seuil, Paris, 2009.

Gendrin, Catherine, *Les Contes de l'olivier*, Rue du Monde, Paris, 2007.

Gotschaux, Étienne, *Dictionnaire pratique et commenté du judaïsme*, Palio, Paris, 2011.

Gougaud, Henri, *Le livre des chemins*, Albin Michel, Paris, 2009; *L'Arbre à soleils*, Points Seuil, Paris, 1979.

Green, Arthur, *La Sagesse dansante de rabbi Nahman*, Albin Michel, Paris, 2000.

Greenbaum, Avraham, *Le Jardin des âmes*, Breslov Research Institute, Paris, 1985.

Kahn Michèle, *Contes et légendes de la Bible*, Pocket Jeunesse, Paris, 1994.

Klein-Zolty, Muriel, *Contes et récits humoristiques du monde juif*, L'Harmattan, Paris, 1991.

Koskas, Sonia, *Chlimou qui parlait aux oiseaux*, L'Harmattan, Paris, 2007.

Korczak, Janusz, and LIFTON, Betty Jean, *Le Roi des enfants*, Robert Laffont, Paris, 1989.

Leyb Cahan, Yehuda, *Contes populaires yiddish*, Imago, Paris, 2009.

Malka, Victor, *Les Plus Belles Légendes juives*, Points Seuil, Paris, 1998; *Proverbes de la sagesse juive*, idem, 1994; *Dieu comprend les histoires drôles*, idem, 2008; *Petites Étincelles de sagesse juive*, Albin Michel, Paris, 2005.

Ouaknin, Marc-Alain, *Tsimtsoum,* Albin Michel, Paris, 1992; *Méditations érotiques* and *Concerto pour quatre consonnes sans voyelles,* Payot, Paris, 2003 and 1998.

Pavlát, Léo, *Contes Juifs,* Gründ, Paris, 1986.

Rabbi Nahman of Bratslav, *Songes, énigmes et paraboles,* Bibliophane-Daniel Radford, Paris, 2002.

Regnot, Franz, *Contes de rabbi Na'hman de Breslev,* translated from the Yiddish, Breslov Research Institute, 1985.

Rosten, Léo, *Les Joies du yiddish,* Calmann-Lévy, Paris, 1994.

Soulier, Jacques, *Du serment d'Hippocrate à l'éthique médicale,* thesis on medicine (about Maimonides), Marseilles, 1985.

Weill, Arthur, *Contes et récits juifs à travers les siècles,* Comptoir du livre du Keren Hasefer, Paris, 1958.

Wiesel, Elie, *Célébration hassidique,* Seuil, Paris, 1972.

Zimet, Ben, *Contes des sages du ghetto,* Seuil, Paris, 2003.

Acknowledgments

For Fanny Walberg for her comments.

For Tevye, Tzvi Fishman's magnificent hero.

For the gentle brother wearing a talith,
with gratitude.

Photo credits

AKG, Paris: IAM/World History Archive: 10; Eric Lessing: 33, 123 (detail) (2); akg-images: 80, 94–95, 141, 172–173; Sotheby's: 127.

BNF, Paris: 16, 36 (detail), 49 (detail), 55, 85, 101 (detail), 138, 149, 150 (detail) (2), 151 (detail), 152 (detail), 153 (detail), 165 (detail), 184 (detail), 186 (detail), 195.

Bridgeman Giraudon: The Israel Museum, Israel/Gift of Mr. Rubin, Amsterdam: 2–3 and 192, 234–235; © Cheltenham Art Gallery and Museums, Gloucestershire, UK: 58; Private collection/Photo Bonhams, London, UK: 97, 160–161, 168–169; British Library, London, UK/© British Library Board, All rights reserved: 12, 105; Musée Bonnat, Bayonne, France/Giraudon: 110; Pushkin Museum, Moscow, Russia: 130; Leeds Museums and Galleries, UK: 154.